A REVOLUTIONARY WAR NOVEL

CHRISTOPHER HAWKINS
and his Daring Escapes

JEANNE BROWNLEE BECIJOS

Adapted and Expanded from Christopher Hawkins' Memoir
The Adventures of Christopher Hawkins

Christopher Hawkins and His Daring Escapes

Copyright @ 2023 by Jeanne Brownlee Becijos

This fictionalized novel is adapted and expanded from Christopher Hawkins' *Adventures of Christopher Hawkins,* first published in 1864.

Book Design by Rebecca Barney

Formatted by Staci Olsen

staciolsen.com

Torch Publications, California

ISBN: 978-0-911079-03-6 (Hardcover)

ISBN: 978-0-911079-02-9 (Paperback)

To seekers of truth and freedom

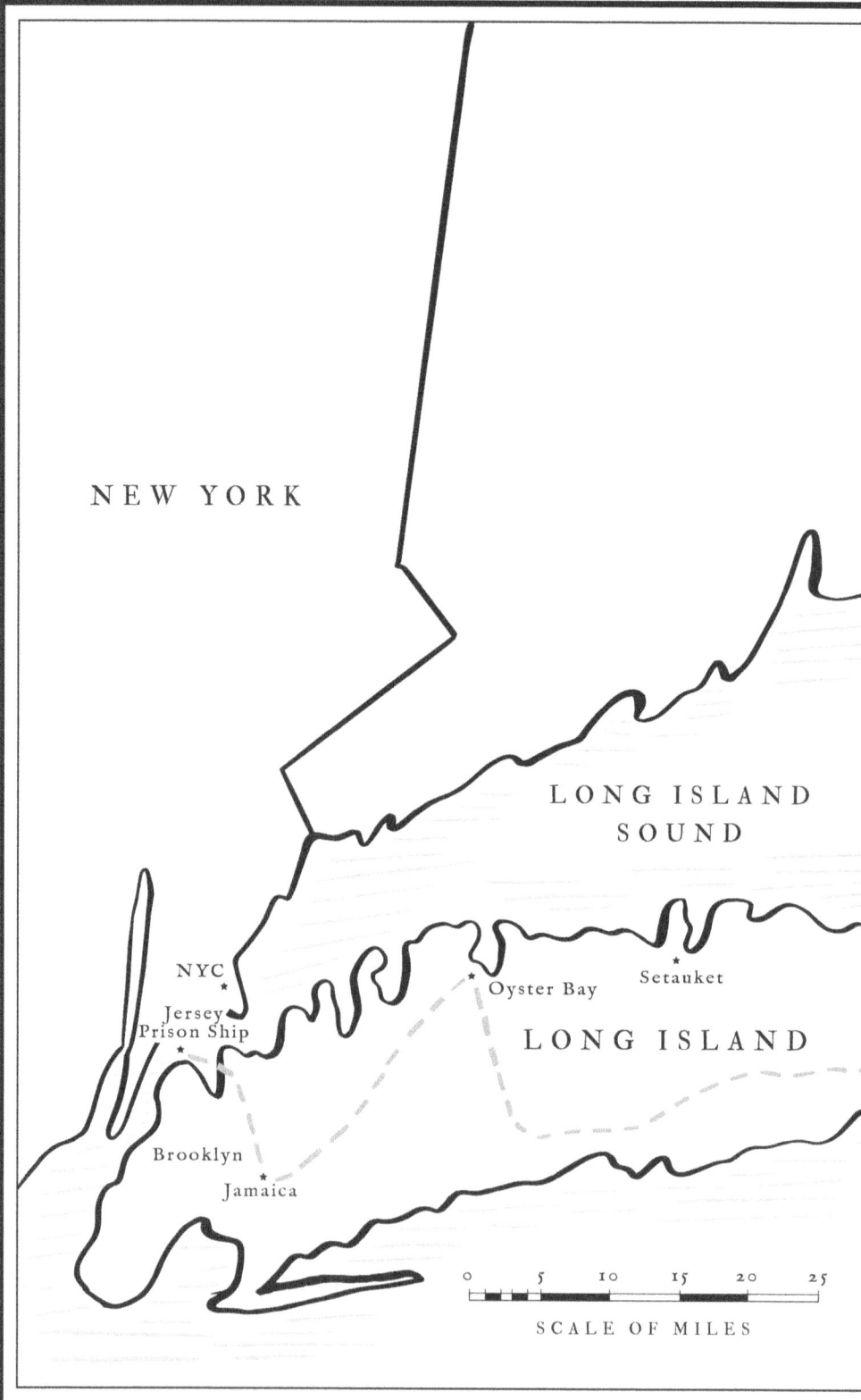

NEW YORK

LONG ISLAND
SOUND

NYC
Jersey
Prison Ship

Oyster Bay   Setauket

LONG ISLAND

Brooklyn
Jamaica

0   5   10   15   20   25

SCALE OF MILES

RHODE
ISLAND

CONNECTICUT

Providence ★

Stonington ★

Sag Harbor ★

ATLANTIC
OCEAN

Christopher Hawkins'
Escape Route

CHAPTER 1
May 4, 1776

Providence, Rhode Island

The darkness was absolute. Wooden walls pressed against my shoulders, head, and feet. I wiggled and squeezed my knees closer to my chest. There was some room to move, but not much.

How long could I last inside this barrel? Maybe a few days. My biggest problem was the lack of water. In time, my skin would shrivel, and my dry tongue would choke me.

Once we were miles from the harbor, though, I could escape my prison. I'd climb out of the barrel and present myself to the sea captain. "Sir, I know I'm a stowaway, but I'll work hard to serve America." The captain might frown and give me a whack, but he'd be pleased to have another hand on deck.

My stowaway boat was anchored in Providence Harbor. Raising the barrel lid, I breathed in the fresh, salty air and watched gray ocean waves disappear into the horizon. It was my destiny to become a sailor.

"You rascal, what are you doing in there?" A rough hand yanked me by the ear out of the barrel. I tumbled to the deck. A sailor with powerful arms raised his foot to kick me, but I rolled out of the way.

"I wasn't trying to stow away, I promise." At least not today —maybe in a few months.

"You little urchin." He lurched forward to grab me, but I scrambled to my feet. The seaman grunted. "I'll have you put in the pillory and then throw rotten eggs at you."

Racing like a rabbit, I sped down the ship's plank and into the town of Providence. I zigzagged around a farmer hauling a cart of turnips and almost tripped a woman in a fine blue dress. "Sorry." I glanced behind, but no one was following me. I made my way to the boat belonging to my friend's uncle. It was an aging forty-five-foot sloop with one mast and two sails.

My blond friend yelled from the edge of the boat. "Christopher Hawkins, where were you?"

"I was practicing stowing away on that ship." I pointed to the vessel.

"What! You're a ninnyhammer. Help carry these boxes to my uncle's. Hurry, the sun's setting."

I climbed on board. Josiah and I carried the heavy boxes down the plank and onto the cobblestone street. We made our way through the crowd and passed two rich merchants with their big bellies and sharp noses in the air.

Loud shouts came from a group of men in the middle of the street. Josiah and I halted. "What's going on?"

Waving a pistol in the air, a gigantic man shouted, "Rhode Island is free!"

The men cheered, threw their tri-cornered hats in the air, and slapped one another on the back. "Huzzah! Huzzah!"

Josiah called to a man who was waving a beer tankard. "Sir, what happened?"

"Today the colony of Rhode Island has renounced its allegiance to Great Britain," the man proclaimed.

I let out a whoop. "Down with King George!" Father always complained about England's ruler.

A copper-haired man faced the crowd. "We are the first colony to break away. When will our fearful neighbors join us?"

"Rhode Islanders, prepare to fight for liberty." A white-wigged, heavyset man shook his raised fist. Passersby joined the joyous group. They were laughing and jostling one another. Two men stood their distance from the others and scowled.

I gave a whoop. "I can't wait to tell Father the news. He's been growling about the King for years."

Josiah laughed. "Look at you. You're red-faced and breathing like you won a race. I think you have Patriot Fever."

"We both do. I know you want to capture British ships."

My friend grinned and nodded his agreement.

We walked to a small wooden house near the wharf. Once inside his uncle's home, Josiah and I sat next to the hearth.

Josiah's uncle, a big man in a weathered jacket, entered the room. Captain Greene's leathery face spoke of his life at sea. "Hello, boys." He sat down in a large chair. "I have good news for you, Josiah. This afternoon I spoke with Commodore Whipple. Since you're almost 14 years old, you may join his ship as a cabin boy. He expects to sail in a month or two."

"Wonderful! I'll be part of the Continental navy." Josiah jumped up and danced a jig, his yellow hair flying in all directions.

I grabbed the captain's arm. "Can I be a cabin boy, too?"

The man gave a rusty laugh. "You want to sail with Josiah?

The two of you would make more mischief than a shipload of monkeys."

"Please, sir. Will you ask Commodore Whipple about me?" I searched for my answer in the captain's eyes.

The captain took a few moments to light his pipe and puff on it. "With your father's permission, I'll check with the Commodore."

I whooped and joined Josiah in a jig. "I'm going to be a Patriot in the navy! Watch out, redcoats, we're after you. We'll steal your cargo and send you home crying to your king."

Josiah grinned at me. "We'll make a deadly twosome."

The captain placed his hand on my shoulder. "Hurry on home, Christopher, or you'll stumble in the dark."

Josiah handed me a bucket. "Thanks for your help today. Here's some fish for your family."

I headed home as the darkness gathered around me. Inside the pail of fish, the glassy eye of a sea bass gave an accusing look. "No need to glare at me like that. I know I'm late for supper."

A half-moon rose above the horizon on my last mile to North Providence. The light helped me avoid ruts and rocks on the dirt road. Father would be angry at my tardiness. I rubbed my behind, prepared for a birch stick beating. But what did it matter? I was going to serve Rhode Island.

First, though, I needed Father's permission. And that wouldn't be an easy task.

CHAPTER 2
May 1776

I peeked through our window and saw that supper was finished. I decided not to ask Father's permission until he was smoking his pipe near the fire and my seven brothers and sisters were in bed. Ma would not be pleased with my news, but surely Father would be proud of me. I'd be fighting to win Rhode Island's freedom.

I stepped inside our home. Eight-year-old Stephen studied by the fire while ten-year-old Mary played with the five little ones. Stephen looked like my father, with his sharp nose and brown eyes. Mary and I favored our mother, as we had black hair and blue eyes. In her white cap and dark shawl, Ma washed dishes while Father stirred the fire in the hearth.

Little Luther clapped his chubby hands. "Cwistofer's home!"

"Ma, I have fish for us." I held up my pail as I entered the room, hoping she'd forgive my lateness.

"Thank you, Christopher." Ma patted my cheek and took the fish from me.

Father didn't speak. The deep lines around his mouth gave him a permanent frown. My father motioned me to sit next to him. His bushy eyebrows almost hid his stern eyes. "Your tardiness shows me you are not responsible."

"I'm sorry, Father. But have you heard about the glorious proclamation from our General Assembly?"

My mother wagged her finger at me. "Don't let the little children hear of this. It will scare them."

With a hint of a smile, my father nodded. "Yes, I did hear the news, but we'll obey your mother's wishes and not discuss the matter."

My desire to join the Continental navy bubbled inside of me, ready to explode. I bit my tongue but could not hold back any longer. "Father, I have a serious question to ask you." I took a deep breath and exhaled quickly. "Captain Greene said he'll help me find a position as a cabin boy. I'll support the Sons of Liberty in the navy, but only with your permission. May I, Father? Please? It's a great honor. And I've always dreamed of sailing the ocean."

Father grunted at me. "Absolutely not."

"Christopher Hawkins, I'll never permit you to be a sailor." My mother waved a wooden spoon at me. "The sea is too dangerous. Only last month, five local fishermen died in a storm."

My father stood up and towered over me. "Son, you think war is a child's game. Your head is filled with fantasies about its glory."

No. The answer was no. A cold pain started in my chest and spread throughout my body. My dream of being a sailor in the navy was shattered. "But Father—"

"Besides, I have other plans for you." My father sat down, and his eyes bore into mine. "I have arranged an apprenticeship for you. You are bound out to Mr. Aaron Mason, a tanner."

All my muscles tensed. I knew well of Mr. Mason's place near the river. Several times I'd accompanied my father there to deliver our cowhides to be transformed into leather. With its odor of dead cows and tanning vats, the tannery smelled ten times worse than any business in Providence. "You want me to make leather at that foul-smelling place? Father, I don't want to work at a tannery."

"The matter is already settled. You'll go live with Mr. Mason on your twelfth birthday next month." Father clapped his hands on his legs. "You'll stay with him until you turn 18. Mr. Mason will teach you a trade, and you will work for him in exchange."

"But Father, a tanyard? You can smell that awful place from miles away." My mind swirled, and my stomach sickened. There had to be a way to escape this horrid apprenticeship.

My father pounded his fist into his palm. "You are the eldest. You shall set an example for the others."

I ignored the warning signals of my father's growing anger. Without a thought, my words tumbled out. "Father, I refuse to be a tanner's apprentice."

Father shook his fist at me. "Do you want to land in jail? I have already signed the legal papers." My father filled the small room with his rage.

Matching his anger with my own, I yelled, "Why didn't you ask me first what I wanted?"

"How dare you show disrespect to your father?" He raised his hand to strike me, but Mother moved between us.

"Hezebiah, don't." Mother trembled. She never spoke up

against my father. "Please, I beg you." Tears rolled down her pale cheeks like dew on a white rose.

Stephen's thin shoulders shook, and Mary gathered the little ones around her. James and Lydia were crying, upset by the loud voices.

"To bed, all of you!" My father's voice thundered through the room.

My head down, I slunk to the small room and bed I shared with three of my brothers.

I felt as if I was being smothered beneath a load of rocks. The life my father had chosen for me was unbearable.

I could follow my father's wishes and become an apprentice at a foul-smelling tannery. Or, I could run away.

CHAPTER 3
May-June 1776

My sleeping brothers beside me didn't stir as I tossed and turned. Should I run away? In the middle of the night, I made my decision. I had to escape my terrible situation. First, I would grab my belongings when Father was away from the house. I could find food on my long journey by eating berries and asking farmers for food. It might take a few days to walk to Newport, but I could do it. Once there, I would find a captain willing to take on a willing and strong young man like myself.

A rooster crowed, and a ray of sun came through the window. In the light of day, my brave thoughts collapsed. No captain in the navy would take me at my young age.

During the next few days, I swam in my gloom. I saw my future as an endless line of dark and cheerless days. I learned that Ma was to have another child. We barely had enough food for our family now. At least there would be one less mouth to feed when I was gone.

A week before the start of my apprenticeship, Josiah came to visit. I stopped pitching hay to greet him when he led his brown bay horse inside the barn.

Josiah's chest thrust upward with pride. "In three weeks, I'm to set sail under Commodore Abraham Whipple on the *Columbus*."

I didn't respond. Josiah had the good fortune to go to sea while I was to be thrown into a deep vat of tanning acid.

Josiah's smile drooped at the edges. "Aren't you pleased?"

I didn't want him to see my bitterness, so I forced a light tone. "Of course. With your yellow hair, your commander will use you to light the way at night."

Josiah grabbed my pitchfork and pretended to fight me. When I didn't respond, he put down the tool. "I should say goodbye to everyone."

Since he only had his uncle, we were like a second family to Josiah. I put the pitchfork in the corner and led my friend into the house.

At our entrance, little Lydia shrieked, "Josiah is here!" My seven brothers and sisters crowded around my friend like ants swarming on a spilled drop of blueberry jam.

"Josiah has joined the navy," I said to my family.

Ten-year-old Mary's cornflower blue eyes grew as big as tea saucers. "No, you can't go to war. What if you are injured? Or worse?"

"Wish me luck. Your words will protect me." Josiah smiled at my sister.

Mary froze in place while her eyes flooded with tears. Then she gave Josiah a fierce hug.

My mother's face was as white as the first November snow. "I'll pray for you every day."

Before Josiah left, I spoke to him outside. "Attack those redcoats until they are blue in the face."

"I will." Josiah grinned at me. "You won't have me to guide

you any longer. Remember to think before you leap. You're good at finding trouble."

"It's a shame you'll no longer be part of my fine adventures." I paused, and my voice became unsteady. "I'll join you as soon as I am able. Father can't keep me away from the sea forever."

June 4TH, 1776, was the day of my twelfth birthday. It was time to say goodbye to my family.

Lydia grabbed onto my legs and wailed. "Christopher, don't go. Don't leave me." The heads of Mary and Stephen drooped so low I could not see their faces. The little ones cried while Father was the only one in the family with dry eyes. Teardrops crept down my face, but I was quick to brush them away.

My mother handed me a folded cloth filled with a potato roll, chicken, and a pickle. "You never know what food they'll give you."

I rode with my father to Mr. Mason's tannery, which was seven miles north of Providence. I felt I was leaving a peaceful land behind me and entering the kingdom of a wretched ogre.

Along the way, Father said, "I've decided to join Rhode Island's troops in a month or two."

I didn't respond. I was the one who should be fighting while he stayed home to protect our family.

The tanyard had a stream running alongside it. We were a half-mile away when I first smelled the place. The foul stench stung my nostrils. There were no more farms or houses. No one wished to live near a tannery.

"You will do well here. Is that not right, son?"

I nodded, but my heart sank. I faced six years of smelly, filthy labor until I was set free.

Within the tanyard, eight men and one boy near my age were working. Deep in the ground sat a dozen rectangular pits, each the length of a man. The two rows of pits were partly covered by a shelter. More than twenty cow, ox, and horse hides dried on wooden racks.

"Mr. Mason, this is my oldest child, Christopher." My father shook hands with the tannery's master. "I am certain you will be satisfied with him. My son is strong and not afraid of a day's work."

A compliment from my father? I almost looked to see if my brother Stephen was nearby.

My father added, "Feel free to punish the boy if he steps out of line."

Mr. Mason crossed his hands over his broad stomach. "We all work hard here. He'll learn to do as I say." The coldness of his gray eyes hinted he was a man with little humor. "Ezekiel, my overseer, will guide him in his tasks."

"Goodbye, Christopher." My father gave me a nod.

"Goodbye, Father." I watched him ride away, sitting tall in his saddle. He didn't look back, not even once.

"Come with me, lad." Ezekiel slapped me hard on the back of my head. "None of us workers stand around gawking."

Ezekiel, a muscular man with a scarred black hole in place of his left ear, showed me around the tannery. "After the hides are washed, they are placed in a lime solution to loosen the hair. Then we scrape off the hair and flesh in the shed." Two men with two-handled knives were scraping hair and fat from the hides. "The next step is to put the hides in pits of tannin. The tannin keeps the hide from rotting." Ezekiel pointed to a bald man stirring the contents of a vat. "We keep the hides in the pits for as long as a year before they become proper leather."

The overseer had scars on his hands and arms, a sight that made me cringe. Was this my fate from laboring here? Ezekiel led me to the racks on the edge of the tanyard. I kept my distance from a stack of wet hides that smelled like rotting flesh.

"We give you boys the work that requires muscle but no brains," said Ezekiel with a snort. Ezekiel jerked his thumb at a thin lad who was thumping hides on the racks. "This is Billy. I hope you learn faster than that lad."

Billy gave me a big, crooked grin.

Ezekiel breathed in the rotting smell of the hides, smiling as if he enjoyed it. "You understand the process? Or did my explanation fall out of a hole in your head?"

"Of course, I understand." I didn't care for Ezekiel's meanness. Besides, he was the one with the hole in his head, not me.

Ezekiel pointed to a dark-skinned man with thick arm and leg muscles. "David will show you your work. Mind you, boy, do what you're told, so you don't get a taste of my rod." Ezekiel laughed and gave me a cruel look. "David, show this green lad how to rinse the new hides."

David led me to a wagon loaded with fresh hides. "What's your name, boy?" The man had a soft voice in contrast to his strong build.

I stood tall. "I'm Christopher Hawkins."

"Carry that hide to the stream over there."

Lifting a hide from the stack, I nearly fainted from the hideous smell. The cowhide still had blood, ooze, and manure on it. I staggered to the side of the stream with the hide. There was a board that crossed the narrow stream.

David said, "Stand on the board and use this pole to move the skin in the stream. You want to remove blood and dirt."

"How long do I do this?"

David smiled. "Give it a few hours for now. It will take several days to be ready."

Groan. Again and again, I brushed the hide against the rocks and swirled it in the water. My mind grew numb. Six years at this mindless labor, and I would have the brain of a three-year-old.

The stream below me was thick with blood, hair, and flesh. I saw a worker dump a tub of foul liquid into the water. I pitied the people down the road who drank from the stream. After an hour, my arms, back, and legs were numb with effort.

While I labored, I saw Billy carrying a tub of chicken dung to a vat. When Billy had his head turned, I saw Ezekiel stick out his leg and trip the boy. The tub spilled, and Billy fell headfirst into the manure. Billy cried out and ran to the stream to wash his face.

"That Ezekiel is as mean as a wild hog, isn't he?" I said to the boy.

Billy wiped the dung from his eyes. "I don't like Ezekiel. I don't like him one bit."

That evening Ezekiel and the other men left for their homes. Mr. Mason motioned to me. "Come inside, boys. Christopher, you'll eat supper in the kitchen with Billy."

My hunger grew threefold at the spread of roast beef, rolls, and four different vegetables, a true feast. I sat down, grabbed a fork, and speared a slab of meat.

A little older than myself, the girl serving our food was rosy-cheeked. "Call me Fanny. You are Christopher, they tell me. Do you like it here?" The girl's wide smile showed her tiny teeth.

"It will do," I answered.

She stared at me. "You have the bluest eyes I have ever seen. Or maybe your black hair makes them seem so blue." Smelling of sweet sweat, Fanny leaned closer to me.

"I'm finished, thank you." It'd be wise to keep a safe distance from Fanny. She appeared too eager to find a husband. I was years away from such a fate.

Billy and I slept in a shed that was attached to the house. The small area was crowded with our two sleeping pallets and a crate for clothes. I felt a pain in my heart when I thought of my family getting ready for bed. They were only a few miles away, but I might as well be halfway to the moon. Exhausted from the labor, I had no trouble falling asleep.

A rooster's call awakened me. I didn't remember where I was until I smelled the stench of rotting flesh and wet hides. I vomited into the pail near my bed.

After breakfast, I joined the other laborers already at work. Ezekiel grunted at me and pointed to the stream. I sighed. Another day of washing hides. When my work was finished, I watched the men at work in the shed. I learned the tools they used and fetched and cleaned them as needed.

The labor was hard and monotonous. One day, David showed me how to stir the hides in the vats. Under his direction, I took a pole and began to stir.

David pointed to the liquid. "Be careful not to splash the harsh solution on you or breathe in the vapors. It can cause eye and lung damage. An apprentice fell in a liming vat two years ago and died."

I shook my head in misery. So, this was my life for the next few years.

In mid-July, I awoke to a commotion outside. I threw on my clothes and rushed to the yard. The workers gathered around Nate, a bald man who shouted in excitement.

"They've done it." Nate slapped his head in delight.

"What?" asked David.

"All the colonies are now free of England!" Nate did a quick jig in the yard. "General Washington and the Continental Congress signed a Declaration of Independence."

I clapped my hands and hollered at the good news. "We'll chase those British buffoons out of America."

Joseph, an older man, sniffed as he continued to sharpen his blade. "We're not free yet."

I whistled a tune. And the British called us Yankee doodles? We'd show them. America was now an independent country. With any luck, the war would be over in a few months. Not too quickly, though, I hoped—not before I joined the navy.

In the tanyard, Ezekiel yelled at Billy. "You ruined this piece of leather! You are a worthless worm." He seized Billy by the pants and threw him into a liming pit.

"Help! The lime is burning me." Billy splashed the water frantically like a frightened baby in a bath. He tried to climb out of the pit but slipped and fell back into the water.

What if Billy died? "I'll get you out. Stay still." Turning my head to avoid the spray of the liming solution, I reached for Billy's arms. Billy frantically grabbed me, causing me to fall headfirst into the pit. I squeezed my eyes tight, hoping not to be blinded by the liquid. Struggling, I pulled Billy and myself out of the pit.

Ezekiel laughed at the two of us. "You two buffoons. You're playing in clean water. We haven't put limestone in that pit yet."

The man delighted in torturing Billy and me. I feared I'd wallop Ezekiel with my fists the next time he tormented Billy and me.

CHAPTER 4
May 1777

I was nearing my one-year anniversary of working at the tannery. How I hated my apprenticeship. The fumes from the pits were choking me, and my hands were stained brown and orange. Burns crisscrossed my arms. I was boiling over with anger, like an untended pot over the fire.

At breakfast, Fanny handed me a newspaper. "Christopher, here is the Boston Gazette. I know you can read." She smiled at me.

I waited until that evening to read the Gazette. One of the notices caught my eye.

AN INVITATION TO ALL BRAVE SEAMEN AND MARINES WHO HAVE AN INCLINATION TO SERVE THEIR COUNTRY AND MAKE THEIR FORTUNES

A grand Privateer ship will Sail on a Cruise against the Enemies of the United States of America. This therefore is to invite all those Jolly Fellows—who love their country and want to make their fortunes at one Stroke—to go immediately to the Wharf. They will be received with a hearty Welcome.

I didn't understand every word but figured out the main idea. The liquor of patriotism flowed through my veins. If only I were older and could join those brave men.

In our sleeping quarters, Billy saw me reading the paper. "What does it say?"

"It's a notice inviting men to sail on a privateer."

"A privateer?"

"It's a private ship, so the sailors take a part of the prize."

Billy shivered. "Are they pirates?"

"No, not at all. Privateers capture enemy ships and share the profits with our country."

Perhaps when I turned fourteen, I'd sail on a privateer. The seamen on private merchant ships were paid many times the salary of sailors in the Continental navy. I could bring home money for my mother.

The next day, David began coughing so hard that his face turned purplish. He staggered and landed heavily on a bench. He coughed and spat blood on the ground.

Ezekiel stared at the man. "How long have you felt sick?" he asked.

David struggled to speak. "For two days."

"You'd best go home. Joseph, help the man."

I watched as the men left the yard. Ezekiel muttered under his breath.

David didn't return to work. Five days later, he died.

The men were arriving at the tanyard when we heard the news. "I can't believe David is gone. Only a few days ago, he was healthy and working hard," said Nate.

Joseph shook his head. "He was gone within a week of falling ill with the tanner's sickness."

Ezekiel grunted. "The poor man."

"I pray to God I don't leave Earth in that way. David suffered mightily." Nate wiped his eyes.

Joseph's face was gloomy. "That's two men gone within a year. Archibald died of the cough last spring."

I held my head in my hands. David was always kind to me. I would miss him terribly.

That night I slept for only minutes at a time. I feared my apprenticeship at the tannery was going to kill me.

I examined my choices. I could stay in my apprenticeship and possibly die from the tanner's sickness. Another possibility was I could run away. If caught, I'd be punished for breaking a contract. No doubt I would be flogged and thrown into prison. My father would never forgive me for breaking the law.

But if I wasn't caught, I was free.

It was time to start my adventures at sea. I was only twelve years of age, a month short of thirteen years. No captain in the Continental navy would accept me as a sailor, but perhaps a ship needed a cabin boy. Or maybe I could join a privateer.

I imagined myself on a ship deck, searching the open horizon for an enemy vessel. My two dreams in life were joining into one, like a seaman's knot twisting into place. It was time for me to become a sailor and a Patriot.

CHAPTER 5

Summer 1777

Once I made my decision, I started moving. It was ten o'clock at night, and everyone in the household was sound asleep. In a letter to my mother, I wrote I'd bring money to her soon. I wrote another letter to the master and mistress, apologizing for my actions. In explanation, I told of my desire to serve the American cause. I asked them to say farewell to Fanny and Billy for me but refrained from adding a profane comment about Ezekiel. I left the two letters on my pallet and put my clothes in my knapsack. By Billy's bed, I placed a licorice candy.

Around midnight, I grabbed some food from the kitchen. A board creaked beneath my foot. What if Mr. Mason heard and burst through the door while waving his pistol? No noises came from his bedroom. In a flash, I was out the door.

I escaped from the Mason house to start the biggest adventure of my life.

For three or four miles, I ran down the road in the dark, cloudy night. Branches grabbed my shirt, and I twisted my ankle on a loose rock. Exhausted, I collapsed under an ash tree hidden from the road. I slept until the sun rose above the trees.

After walking two more miles, I found myself in Providence harbor. It was a cloudy May morning with a brisk wind. Rich merchants crossed the cobblestone road. Boys pushed carts filled with cloth, potatoes, or smelly fish. Little children barely escaped being crushed as they wandered in front of a cart or a carriage. Women of wealth wore fashionable hats and silk dresses that cost more than my family's supply of food for a year.

While I was heading toward the dock, I stepped on the hem of an elegant woman's dress by mistake. I bowed and told her, "M'lady, I apologize." The man at her side whacked me on the head with the back of his hand. "Away, you clumsy oaf."

At the waterfront, I felt my heart push against my ribs. I breathed deeply, delighting in the salty, fishy, and spicy smells, the aroma of adventure. Small and large vessels filled the crowded harbor.

I approached a sailor with six months of dirt layered on him. "Excuse me, sir, is there a privateer in the harbor looking for men?"

The seaman examined my fresh face and my height. "Are you asking for your father?"

"No, for myself. I want to serve Rhode Island."

"A boy like you?" The man shook his head and chuckled. "There is a vessel leaving out of New Bedford in the next day or two, but nary a one from this harbor."

"How might I get to New Bedford from here?"

"If I were but a lad, I'd sneak onto that ship over there. She is heading to New Bedford."

The sailor pointed to a merchant vessel. Sailors were loading barrels onto her. Without a second thought, I squeezed myself between two of the men walking up the gangplank. Once on deck, I heard a familiar, dreaded voice.

"Anyone seen a young black-haired boy asking for work?" It was Ezekiel talking to a group of sailors standing at the wharf. "The brainless boy has run away from his apprenticeship."

Even though Ezekiel was several feet away, I was certain he could hear my heart pounding. I crept down narrow stairs to the hold and hid behind barrels of salted cod. I remained there shaking in fear. At last, I heard the noises of the ship departing. I was leaving Ezekiel behind.

After a while, I fell asleep. I didn't know we had landed until a sailor yanked me by my ear and forced me to my feet.

"What rascal is this I spy? A free passage you seek? I'll give you a free passage with my shoe." The gruff sailor forced me to leave the boat with some help from his foot. I fell forward on the dock and landed on my knees. Ow, his kick to my bum hurt.

I had now traveled the farthest of my life. New Bedford, a small harbor in Massachusetts, was forty miles from Providence. I asked the whereabouts of a privateer and was directed to a schooner named the *Eagle*.

Once I found the schooner, I gave her an appraising look. She had five sails and was about 50 feet long. The ship mounted twelve small carriage guns. At the base of the gangplank, there was a line of men. An officer told the sailors to make their mark on his list before they boarded.

I joined the line. When it was my turn, the officer asked, "What is it you fancy, lad? I know you are not on my list." The seaman wore a cocked hat, a blue jacket, and white pantaloons that ended below his knees.

"I want to protect my home of Rhode Island against the British and make a shilling or two in the process."

The officer grinned. "And how old might you be?"

"I am fourteen." I stretched my height as much as I could. It was only a year and a month until I was that age.

"Is that so?" He arched a thick brown eyebrow. "And what will your parents say?"

"I am an orphan." I felt sinful lying about my family, but I was desperate to join the *Eagle*.

"We could use another cabin boy. Are you smart enough for the task?"

"I know my letters and the multiplication table. I plan to learn the Declaration of Independence, and I know—"

"I believe you. Put your mark here. I am your boatswain, Mr. John Ward. Welcome to the *Eagle*, under Captain Mowry Potter. Report to me once we are underway."

I signed my name and marched up the gangplank to the ship's deck.

The boards beneath me creaked, and the vessel swayed. Fire filled my chest, and I suspected smoke was coming out of my nostrils. My life's desire was finally realized. Of course, I knew nothing of a seafaring life, but I was ready to learn.

As we readied to leave port, I watched the crew of about thirty men leap into action. Men scrambled up the masts and rigging and loosened the sails. Gradually we sailed away from the harbor. I saw people turn into insects and buildings into toys. After the vessel was beyond sight of land, she seemed to be steering in the same direction as when she left the harbor. An illusion, I suspected. Soon there was nothing but open water in all directions. The freedom of the ocean! It was as glorious as I had always hoped.

I stood by the ship's side until the sun, like an orange lump of coal, sunk below the horizon. I had never seen a sunset on the ocean before. I much preferred it to the sooty sunsets I saw at the tanyard.

After we were well at sea, I reported to Boatswain John Ward. I found him on the deck. "At your service, sir," I said, saluting the officer.

"There you are. Tell me your name again." Unlike the other officers, he wore his brown hair pulled back in a queue, without a powdered wig.

"I am Christopher Hawkins, ready to carry out your orders, sir."

"Good." The man had a pointed nose and appeared to be ever on the lookout for a bad scent.

"And what will I be doing, sir?" I asked.

"Carrying messages, helping the cook, cleaning up messes, or anything needed. Eli, show this boy around."

"Aye, aye, sir." Eli was a stout seaman, his hairy stomach hanging over the waist of his pantaloons. "Mind you, boy, don't fall overboard. Hold on to a rope or a handle when you are on deck." He poked his finger deep into his nostril and scratched. "Come on, you sluggard, I'll show you your quarters."

We climbed down the ladders to the deck below, where I spied dozens of stowed hammocks. Foul smells hit my nostrils. Eli pointed to a pile of stained bedding. "You claim this one and hang it in a corner tonight. If you die while you are on board, we sew you up in your hammock and toss you overboard to feed the fishes." He laughed at his joke, but I didn't find it funny. "Enjoy your evening. Tomorrow, I'll have you work until you drop."

That night I ate hardtack, which was well-named. Worried I'd break a tooth, I soaked the flavorless biscuit in cider and managed to nibble it. The sailors drank grog, rum mixed with water. After our meal, the crew began singing their sailor ditties.

Eli rubbed his hairy stomach and pointed at me. "Hey, cabin boy, sing along. You'll learn a thing or two."

I joined them with their song about Captain Kidd, the famous pirate:

> *My name is Captain Kidd, as I sailed,*
> *My name is Captain Kidd*
> *And God's laws I did forbid*
> *And most wickedly I did, as I sailed.*
> *My father taught me well*
> *But against him I rebelled, as I sailed,*
> *He shoved a Bible in my hand*
> *But I left it in the sand*
> *And I pulled away from land,*
> *As I sailed.*

As I sang with the crew, I imagined that we were pirates sailing the high seas. It was not that much different. We were after great prizes to be shared by all. The men looked as gruff as the ones I'd seen in drawings of pirates. The main difference was that Captain Potter, with his straight back and well-kept uniform, did not look at all like the sword-waving Captain Kidd.

At night, I hung my hammock. As I climbed into it, the hammock swung completely around and threw me to the floor.

"I think we have a clumsy oaf in our midst," said one of the seamen. The others laughed.

I tried getting in the hammock again, successful this time. Surrounded by loud snoring and overpowering farts, I sought sleep. In time, the swinging hammock calmed me and sent me to slumber.

In the morning, Eli, smelling of day-old rum, shook me awake. "Get your lazy bum on deck." After a bowl of porridge, I was set to labor. I carried messages back and forth across the ship's decks between the officers. Before supper, I was ordered to the galley to help the cook, an immense black man with quick hands. The cook told me, "Slice the potatoes."

I grabbed one of the potatoes and swung my knife. Unfortunately, the knife handle was greasy with oil. The knife slipped out of my hand, and the potato bounced on the floor.

"You jackanape!" yelled the cook, swinging his knife uncomfortably close to my ear. "You have the hands of a cow."

That evening, I served the officers their food in the room on the starboard side. When boatswain Ward spied me, he grabbed my arm. "Mates, here is our young Patriot. Besides knowing the Declaration, I imagine you are also acquainted with General Washington?" There was a twinkle in his eye.

"I spoke to our leader when he visited Providence, but he is not a personal friend." I had snuck away from work to see the great man during his visit to our town.

The officers chuckled. "Then give him our regards next time you meet," said Mr. Ward with a wink.

Captain Potter gave me a nod but no more. He was a serious man who did not joke when the others did. The sun had fried his cracked skin to a deep red.

As I returned to the galley, I saw a youth leaving the area. "Hey there. Who are you?" I asked.

The startled lad glanced from side to side and then answered. "I am cabin boy to the lieutenant. He is my father's cousin." Although the lad was taller than I, he was as thin as a mast pole.

"My name is Christopher, and I'm cabin boy to Boatswain Ward." Perhaps we would be friends during our long voyage.

"I am Paul." His eyes studied the sea-worn deck.

"Why don't we—" Before I could finish my question, Paul skittered away. He reminded me of the rats I had seen scurrying below deck.

In the next few days, I watched Boatswain Ward and the other officers about the ship. I asked the busy boatswain, "What exactly is your job, sir?"

Mr. Ward said, "I make the schedule, oversee the men's work, and make sure this ship stays afloat."

"You seem to be always on the move. The other officers stand about and are careful their powdered wigs and fine uniforms don't get dirty."

Mr. Ward gave a short laugh. "Don't share your observation with the captain if you want to keep your skin."

The *Eagle* was headed to England, with an expected voyage of five weeks or more. Every day we looked for sails on the horizon but were disappointed. The crew was hoping for several prizes along the way. We all wanted our due.

During the first week, sailors caught fish off the Newfoundland coast. We had halibut for a meal. This was a pleasant change to the salted pork.

Hoping to be more than a waiter, I was eager to discover the ways of a ship. I watched in awe as the seamen clambered up and down the masts and rigging and adjusted the sails. "Eli, please let me learn the work of a seaman."

Eli pointed to a rough-looking man with a scar stretching

from his ear to chin. "Killer can show you how to avoid breaking your skinny neck."

Killer stared at me. One of his eyes was bigger than the other, giving him a fierce expression. Although curious, I was afraid to ask the origin of his name. Killer waved me to come closer. "Watch me, boy. See how I place my feet."

I observed as the seaman scrambled up the rigging. Like a wild animal, Killer never paused as he raced to the top of the mast. Gripping the rigging with my toes, I climbed a few feet and then looked down. I could see the bald spot on Eli's head. Losing my balance, I fell to the deck.

Eli sneered at me. "A graceful infant, ain't you?"

I was determined to succeed. Every day I was able to climb higher. Within a short time, I reached the top of the mainmast. The view at the ship's highest point filled my heart with joy. The unending, gray-blue ocean surrounded our ship. We were a pearl in an endless oyster. I was sailing the vast seas, which was my dream since I was little.

Killer taught me to trim the sails. I unfurled them when we needed more power and hauled the sails in when the wind was overly strong.

I kept track of the days. Almost a month into the voyage, I turned thirteen years of age, at peace with my life. I was sailing the high seas, surrounded by an ocean of many moods. Soon we would capture a British ship, and I'd show my worth as a Patriot.

After five weeks and three days, we caught sight of the British Isles. The rocky coast looked similar to our own in America. This was the land of my ancestors and the home of my parents' cousins. It was also the land of our fiercest enemy—a mother turned into a tyrant.

Seeing nothing of interest, the captain stayed on the coast for only a short time. We proceeded to turn back for America. I couldn't believe we had sailed for eight weeks without a single prize. I had promised my mother that I would have money to give her.

After several days on our return voyage, we finally spied a sail. The men slapped one another in glee. I jumped and shouted. Grabbing a spyglass, I saw the ship as clear as day.

A command rang through the air. "Be ready to fire the cannons."

We were about to take our first capture and prize.

CHAPTER 6
Summer 1777

Our vessel chased after the ship in the distance. On approach, we saw she was a schooner with no guns. Lieutenant Paine hailed her. "Ahoy! We are an American vessel. From where do you sail?"

An officer with a foreign accent returned our call. "We are a French vessel from the West Indies, bound for Halifax."

"We will board you. If you stop us, expect an attack from our guns." The men were at the ready to fire our cannons. In response, the schooner lowered her sails and allowed Lieutenant Paine to board. Our crew eyed one another, holding our breaths and praying for a prize.

"I wager that ship is loaded with French perfume." Killer inhaled as if smelling the exotic scent.

"Why not spices and sacks of hard candy?" asked a sailor, who slobbered from the side of his mouth. Myself, I hoped for a chest of gold pieces.

An hour later, Lieutenant Paine reboarded the *Eagle* and shook his head in disappointment. "They are telling the truth. I examined their papers; the ship is French. They are loaded with nothing more than bags of flour."

Mr. Ward, the boatswain, muttered to himself. "You cowards, hiding behind your mothers' skirts." He growled to the captain and Lieutenant Paine, "That ship is British, pretending to be French. The crew is dressed in disguise with French turbans on their heads." Many of the men nodded their agreement. "I say we take the vessel now."

"Step back, Mr. Ward. We're returning to America." The captain's sun-reddened face flushed two shades darker.

I looked between the captain and my master. A storm was brewing.

Shaking his head and cursing under his breath, Mr. Ward returned to his quarters. I followed the boatswain. "Sir, would you like something to eat or drink?"

"No." He threw his shoes against the cabin wall.

"If we captured that vessel and she was truly French, would we be called pirates?" Seeing Ward's scowl, I regretted my boldness. I stepped backward so he wouldn't throw me across the room, as he'd done with his shoes.

After a tense moment, the officer gave a short laugh. "Don't worry, young Hawkins. Mistakes are made in times of war. You won't be hanged. As for myself, I reckon the captain would hang me now if he could."

Back on deck, I could tell by the crew's dark mood that they were furious with the captain's decision.

"We have a bumbling fool for a master." Eli spat a greenish blob on the deck.

I knew not to get the men riled. They looked ready to twist someone's neck like a chicken.

Grumblings and rumblings continued. Three days later, in

the early misty morning, we spied the white sail of a different ship. The captain gave orders to go after her.

Eli growled. "Even if it is a true prize, our worthless officers will not take her."

I hoped that this ship would be our first reward.

After giving chase for several hours, we slowly gained on her. The vessel we followed was a large brigantine: copper-bottomed, British-built, with two masts, and apparently unarmed. We ran up our colors and fired a warning shot at the ship's bow. The vessel did not lower her sails in response. Captain Potter ordered three more guns to fire. Still no response from the brigantine.

The sun was a blurry ball in the hazy sky. "Boatswain, order the crew to sing," said the lieutenant. Pirates used this trick to strike fear in the hearts of their prey. We all joined in a hearty version of "Captain Kidd."

In the darkening twilight, a strong breeze moved our vessel near enough to the brigantine for a broadside. Would we fire our guns? I hoped so.

Our captain hailed the enemy ship. "Ahoy. Where are you heading? Ahoy there."

There was no response. At last, we heard a call from the commander. "Our brigantine is from Liverpool and bound to New York. For heaven's sake, what do you want of us?"

Our crew shouted and slapped one another on the back. We were about to take our first prize! I danced a jig.

"Back your main topsail and shorten your other sails," said Captain Potter. "Then lower your boat and come on board."

Ignoring our captain, the British commander continued the brigantine's course with all sails set.

"Captain, we're in range. Let's broadside her." The lieutenant prepared to fire our guns on the British ship.

"No! What if the brig is armed?" Captain Potter's voice rose to a high pitch. "She would soon blow our little schooner to pieces."

At Potter's lack of action, I heard angry cries from our crew. "What a mouse-livered coward." Eli shook his dagger above his head.

Another man jumped on top of a barrel. "Give command of the *Eagle* to the boatswain. Mr. Ward has more than enough courage to take the brig."

The commander of the brigantine called to our ship. "Would you permit us to lie by you until morning? My boat is lashed fast under my booms, and I cannot get her out. I will board you in the morning."

Captain Potter replied, "Aye, aye."

Our crew was angrier than a Boston mob at the captain's response. Mr. Ward, the boatswain, stalked about and swore like a madman. "That brig will get away from us before morning!" The other seamen agreed. Only the lieutenant and three other officers remained silent.

"It's now dark, and she is most likely armed," said our captain. "Things must remain as they are. I have given my word to lie by her until morning. Now keep a good lookout until then."

"The devil keep a good lookout." Mr. Ward kicked a coiled rope. "We are soon to have a storm." Our sails slapped and flapped in the rising wind. "We must board the brigantine and take possession of her now."

"I command this vessel and will be obeyed." The captain,

his eyes on fire, stood firm.

The boatswain held the captain's eyes, then snorted and walked away. Captain Potter and Lieutenant Paine returned to their quarters.

The crew was bubbling over in anger. Killer jumped on the rigging above us. "Don't let those quaking custards lose our reward! Mr. Ward can lead us."

The crew continued with their angry words about the captain. "Captain Potter is worthless. We need a man with the courage to lead us."

"Men, stop and think," said one of the remaining officers. "You know it is mutiny to take over the ship. It would be a hanging matter for all of you."

After more grumbling, the idea of mutiny was abandoned.

Mutiny was a bad idea. I pictured myself swinging from the gallows, labeled as a traitor, my black tongue sticking out of my head. That did not fit my patriotic plans.

At the earliest morning light, I clambered onto the deck to examine our captured prize. I looked in every direction, but the ocean was gray and empty. The seaman on lookout confirmed my fears. "I've lost sight of the brigantine. She has made her escape from us." Eli cursed and kicked a barrel across the deck. The others joined him in swearing. Familiar curse words and a few new ones flew around me. I didn't have the will to speak.

Captain Potter came on deck in the late morning. "Lieutenant Paine, have you lost sight of the brig?"

"Yes, sir." The lieutenant bowed his head.

Potter accused his officer. "It is blasted strange you could not keep sight of her."

The boatswain turned toward the captain. "It would be

blasted strange if we could," snarled Mr. Ward. "She was using all means to get clear of us."

"Don't be troublesome, Mr. Ward." Captain Potter wore a venomous scowl.

The boatswain stepped forward until he was face to face with the captain. "I speak only for your good and mine."

I feared there might be a duel between them. They were like two swaggering roosters in a battle over a hen. After a few tense moments, the cowardly captain headed for his cabin. He said over his shoulder, "We will continue our return voyage to America."

The next morning, the wind rose to a storm from the northeast. I stood at the rail and watched the huge dark clouds heading our way. A salty spray washed over my body. Killer grabbed my shoulder. "Lad, get away from the rail. Do you want to be swept away?"

The sky opened wide and emptied buckets of rain upon us. Mr. Ward responded immediately. "All hands on deck! Lash the hatches." The crew nailed tarpaulins over the hatches to keep the water from entering the hold below. No one was allowed to leave the deck. With every wave, the sea washed over the vessel from stem to stern and soaked us to the skin. Paul, the timid cabin boy, and I held on to a mast for dear life. Paul's eyes were wide and dark with fear. "Chris—" He yelled, but I couldn't hear him over the thundering of the storm.

The violent gale continued all that day and into the evening. I watched in horror as Killer slipped on the deck and nearly flew over the rail. Luckily, he was able to grab onto a rigging before going overboard.

The storm tossed our ship up high and threw it down in the

water. "We'll sink if this keeps up," said Eli. The grim faces of the crew scared me more than the dark sky. What would happen to us? I imagined my body dragged to the bottom of the sea. The fish and the sand would turn me into an unrecognizable blob. My family could never visit my grave. They wouldn't even know where I was.

The captain called the crew to gather around him. "We need less weight on board. Either twenty of you jump overboard to lighten the load, or we toss some of our guns."

The men groaned, knowing that the loss of cannons would weaken us in battle. "Mr. Ward, direct your men to throw six of our heaviest guns overboard," said the captain. The boatswain was not pleased but followed orders. He must have agreed with the captain's decision.

I felt my stomach growl with hunger, but the wind was too noisy for me to hear. With the hatches lashed shut, we couldn't go below deck to get food.

The entire crew spent the night lashing themselves to the vessel or clinging to the rigging. Killer tied me to the mizzen mast. The saltwater slapped my face. I tried to sleep, but the chill and the violent rocking of the ship kept me awake.

Gray light signaled the second day of the storm. There was nothing to eat or drink above deck except bad water. At this point, we had fasted the whole day and night. A sailor inquired of the captain, "Is there nothing edible in your cabin?"

"Ask the cabin boy. He knows best." The captain waved in my direction.

"There is a bit of food," I said.

"Can you get something to eat if we raise the top of the companionway?" asked a scrawny sailor.

"I'll try." I was willing to search for food. My stomach felt like it was eating itself. While fierce waves washed over me, Eli tied a rope around my waist. One of the crew opened the companionway a foot wide and let me down into the cabin. I gathered all I could find to eat and drink and was hauled up again. The men cheered at my successful efforts as I provided a small meal for each of the crew. I was pleased as a fox after a night in a chicken coop.

During the next dismal and painful night, the gale was vicious. The whiteheads of the waves broke over the deck and kept us awake. On the morning of the third day of the storm, the wind lessened in power, and the water did not break over us as much.

The crew was much dispirited from hunger and fatigue. The lieutenant chose a seaman to enter the vessel's hold to find food. We all cheered when a sailor retrieved food for all.

My share of the food was a hard biscuit and a small piece of raw pork. It was a delicious meal. While devouring my food, memories rushed into my mind. I remembered the last time I had supped with my family. The young ones grabbed my legs when it was time for me to leave.

In a rather melancholy mood, I cast my eyes to search for land. I saw something resembling a small bush without leaves. "Look! I see land or perhaps a ship."

The lieutenant came over and followed my lead. "It's a sail. The vessel is square-rigged under bare poles."

The crew cheered. "She must be that same British brigantine. This time we'll take her."

We made for the ship as fast as wind and weather would

allow. As we approached her, we set more sail. To our horror, the large ship turned around and headed in our direction.

"She's after us!" We shifted our course and changed from a chase to a runaway.

CHAPTER 7
Summer-Fall 1777

O ur efforts to escape the British ship were useless. In moments, the enemy came alongside us. We learned of our ill fate: the English *Sphynx* was a sloop of war with twenty guns.

When she hailed us, our captain answered their call. "We are the American *Eagle,* headed to New Bedford."

"Come under our lee," said the captain of the *Sphynx.*

Confusion and despair spread among our crew.

"We are taken."

"We cannot fight her and keep our lives."

A sailor, who was as short as a boy, wailed in concern. "We'll be put in prison."

What would be my fate as a prisoner? Perhaps starvation, torture, or even death. I had dreamed of prizes and adventure, not of prisons and defeat.

The boats of the *Sphynx* came to carry us to their ship. I was the first to board, anxious to know my fate. My boat was soon loaded with members of our crew and their baggage. When we arrived under the rail of the *Sphynx,* the crew threw ropes to us. I fastened one around my chest and called to those on deck, "Haul away."

A sailor from the quarterdeck answered me. "Put the rope around your neck, you blasted Yankee, and we'll soon bring you up."

The man wanted to hang me!

A British officer on board interfered. "Hurry and haul up the prisoners."

Would the sailors truly hang me? I vowed to keep an eye on this British crew. Even if the officers wanted us alive, one of the devil's sailors could attack me.

Once I landed on deck, my captors encircled me to examine my pewter buttons. A sailor read, "*Liberty and property.* What hogwash." He spat on the button. The motto on my buttons did not suit his taste.

"Get a knife. Cut off those cursed buttons," said a crew member with red hair.

An officer waved the seamen aside. "Leave the boy alone."

The crew did not take the buttons but continued their jokes. I refused to remove the buttons myself. Let the scoundrels jest and stare at me. They didn't understand how Americans felt about liberty. I wasn't going to let their teasing tarnish my patriotism.

Due to the swells of the waves, it took several boat trips to transfer our crew to the British ship. Nothing was removed from the *Eagle*—not a piece of furniture, rigging, tackle, or provision. Once we were all on board, the British fired cannons into our ship. Soon it was exploding with flames. I watched my first ship slowly sink into the ocean, along with my hopes for freedom and a prize.

Our captured crew was put into the cable tier, a part of the hold where cables were stored. Captain Potter, Paul, and I were the only exceptions. Paul was the timid boy I'd seen at the beginning of our voyage. Due to our youth, we cabin boys were given our freedom. Paul and I walked about the decks among the sailors. "Here, Yankees, want some food?" A sailor handed us pork and biscuits.

Paul and I sat on the deck and gobbled down our food. "Can you believe it?" I asked him. "I thought we were going to be tied up and tortured."

My companion shuddered at the thought.

I spoke too soon about our escape from torture. The evening after our capture, the captain of the *Sphynx* ordered Paul and me into a cabin with cannons. The captain, a well-groomed man with a giant bulb for a nose, gave commands to his boatswain's mate. "Tie each boy to a cannon carriage out of each other's hearing."

With a smirk, the mate displayed his whip to us. It was a cat-of-nine-tails. The object had nine cords attached, with two or three knots tied into each tail. I had heard horror stories of this cruel instrument. A beating with a cat-of-nine-tails, capable of exposing muscles and bones, could kill a person.

"God help me!" Paul's thin body shook with fear at the sight of the whip.

The mate first devoted his attention to Paul. After he laid down the whip in full view, the mate tied Paul to the wood frame that supported one of the cannons. In response, Paul made a noise as loud as a crazed bull.

Once the mate secured Paul, he tied me to another cannon. The steel of the gun was cold against my skin. The rope that bound my hands was tight enough to make red marks on my wrists.

The mate sneered at me. "I hope you will not make such cursed crying as your friend does. Then I won't have to whip you."

"If you torture me, I'll be cursed if you make me cry." Except I used another word in place of "cursed." I had begun to learn the sailors' phrases. I tried to sound brave, even though my innards shook within me.

I suspected that the captain wanted information about our vessel and our captures. In a low voice, the captain questioned Paul. The young boy's bawling prevented me from hearing much. The mate snapped his whip through the air and struck Paul's foot. The boy screeched in pain.

At first, Paul only wept, but in time he muttered answers to the captain. I suspected Paul told all since the mate never struck him again with the cat-of-nine-tails.

Now I was put under examination. The captain leaned forward and stuck his bulbous nose in my face. "I want the exact truth from you concerning your cruise."

I was silent. I didn't want to betray my country.

"You better speak, Yankee." The mate's whip whistled through the air and struck the wood near my tied hands.

I had no choice if I wanted to survive. "I shall tell you the truth as far as I know it." Despite my fear, I forced myself to appear confident. The captain asked me a series of questions. I described how Captain Potter allowed a captured British brigantine to run away from us. The British captain and his mate laughed at my comments about Captain Potter.

Once the examination was over, I was untied. The captain

made a honking noise as he blew his enormous nose with an embroidered handkerchief. "You gave us a thorough account. Would you have some wine, boy?"

I rejected his offer. I don't drink alcohol because I prefer to be in control of my thoughts. Besides, I would never drink with the enemy.

That evening I felt guilty about my revelations to the British. I had little respect for our Captain Potter, but he was an American. I reassured myself that I only confirmed Paul's testimony. Besides, I was not interested in a taste of the cat-of-nine-tails.

Our captor kept on her course for America. For the rest of the voyage, Paul and I were allowed our freedom again. After a few weeks, I saw the shores of New York in the early morning light. My whole body warmed to see America again, but my heart soon sank when I remembered I was still a captive.

When we arrived in the port of British-occupied New York City, an officer pointed to an old transport vessel lying near the mouth of the East River. She was stripped of masts, sails, and rigging. "There's your new home, Yankees. You'll join the other stinking rebels." He laughed in our faces.

We were transported to the prison ship.

A mate shoved me onto the deck and into the vessel's hold. In addition to our sailors, hundreds of other American prisoners were already crammed into the hold. My nose and eyes stung with the stench of human waste and disease.

Paul and I pushed our way through the men and made a space for ourselves in the hold. We were given hardtack for food.

"Ugh!" My friend shivered. Worms crawled amid the holes of our biscuits. "How long will they keep us here?"

"I guess until the war is over. That should be any day, I hope." I didn't believe my own words, however. The fighting had already continued for over two years.

After we ate, we clambered over bodies on deck to watch over the rail. In the dusk, the lights of New York City began to twinkle.

"Everyone, down below." A British officer waved his bayonet at us. The guards pushed and shoved the men on deck to descend the stairs. In the hold, there were no benches or hammocks to lie down on. Paul and I squeezed into a small space on the wooden floor, but there was no room to stretch our legs. The redcoats barred the openings. I heard the slamming of locks as they sealed us in the hold.

Paul shoved me. "Christopher, are you awake? I fear I'll have nightmares of being squeezed to death."

"Don't worry, you'll be fine. Dream of mermaids and dolphins."

I acted brave and at peace, but inside I was petrified. I took a deep breath but couldn't get enough air. My arms and legs trembled, and I panted to get more air. To calm myself, I closed my eyes and pictured an endless blue ocean on a clear day.

Three days into our time on the prison ship, an officer brought a newspaper from the city of New York on board. The officer addressed all the captives, close to four hundred in total, including fourteen American captains. "Yankees, listen to this. One of your foolish captains made a donkey of himself. It says that Captain Potter allowed a valuable ship to escape." He proceeded to read the details of the article that ridiculed my captain's conduct. "The vessel that eluded Captain Potter contained fine broadcloth, silks, and salt worth three dollars per bushel."

A prisoner shouted, "You British can have Potter. He don't deserve to be an American." Another sailor from a different ship muttered, "I swear, if I was one of his crew, I'd murder him."

Dejected, Captain Potter lowered his head. His failure was displayed in front of hundreds of Americans. Although I had no respect for our captain, I couldn't help but feel sorry for him.

After I was three weeks on board the prison ship, a British naval officer came in quest of waiters. "Lad, come with me." The officer took Paul by the shoulder and led him away.

"Paul. Paul!" He didn't hear me. I didn't even have a chance to bid farewell to my friend.

Another officer came on board and spoke to me. "I will return in two or three days. You will join us on the British frigate *Maidstone*. She is a fine vessel of twenty-eight guns and 200 men, not one of your Yankee puddle boats." Before he left the ship, Mr. Richards handed me a quarter of a dollar.

I glared at the officer. "No, I won't take it. I won't be paid to enlist in the British service."

Officer Richards threw his hands in the air. "Why you Yankee! This money is to use as you please until I call for you."

I shrugged my shoulders and took the money. The officer went away, chuckling to himself.

Two days later, Mr. Richards came on board. "Hawkins, get ready."

On our way to the frigate *Maidstone*, I noticed her superior appearance to our privateer the *Eagle*. She was large, well-maintained, and had several sails. Although I was unhappy to be held by the British, this vessel was far better than being captive in that appalling, floating prison.

I boarded the large ship that was under the command of Captain Alan Gardner. When I entered the officer's cabin, Mr. Richards motioned me inside. He pointed to an accounting book. "Write your name here."

I stood tall. "No, I shall not sign away my liberty. I prefer to go home and see my mother."

"Don't be foolish. Sign so you can draw wages." At my continued refusal, Mr. Richards said, "I will do it for you, you Yankee."

He signed the book, then closed it with a slam. "I'll call you Chris."

"My Christian name is Christopher."

"But Chris is a good nickname," said the officer. He had the final word, of course.

Mr. Richards kept his quarters in precise order, with a shelf for his powdered wigs and a desk for his maps and papers. I cleaned his cabin and followed his requests. Once I knocked over a bottle of ink from his desk. I feared Mr. Richards would yell or even strike me. "Sorry, sir." I bowed, waiting for my punishment.

"Clean it up, Chris." That was all the officer said to me. I breathed a sigh of relief.

Although I was treated well enough, I never forgot my main goal in life: I had to escape. I didn't want to be in service to the British while my fellow countrymen fought for freedom.

Unfortunately, I never had an opportunity. As summer passed into fall, we never docked near a wharf. If we needed supplies, a boat was sent to shore. Should I jump into the water and swim miles to American land? I decided against this plan. It was far too dangerous.

My master had another waiter in addition to me. Stephen Stone, an English lad from Yorkshire, was three or four years older than me. He had a continuous frown and one hairy eyebrow that crossed his forehead.

I introduced myself. "Hello, Stephen, I'm Christopher Hawkins from Providence, Rhode Island."

The boy spat on the deck. "You blasted Yankee."

That was the beginning and end of any pleasant conversation between us.

Mr. Richards gave Stone little responsibility due to the boy's bad habits. The worst habit was that the youth drank too much rum.

My workload increased due to Stone's laziness. "You were supposed to help in the galley this morning."

Stone raised his mug to me, gulped down the liquid, and burped loudly in my face. The foul smell nearly knocked me over.

I was soon entrusted with Mr. Richards' cabin operations. The officer told Stone to follow my directions as we cooked in the galley and cleaned the cabin. Even though Stone obeyed me in the beginning, after a few weeks he became slow in his response. One morning I was upset with him. "Stone, you didn't clean the master's cabin. Do it now." I commanded the boy for the second time, staying clear of the lad's foul rum breath. The boy slowly turned his head towards the cabin wall and refused to obey. Then he swung his fist and hit me in the stomach.

I gasped. "You brute." I punched his left shoulder. I knew it was against the ship's rules to box, but the lout made me furious.

The lad, taller and broader than I, struck me on the cheek. I hit him four times in a row as he was slow to respond. My last punch knocked him to the ground. Stone grunted and swore but didn't get up.

"What is going on? Chris, why all the noise?" Mr. Richards observed Stone groaning on the floor and my bloody face.

I dreaded the officer's next move. His face was darker than the sea in a violent storm. Was I to be whipped by the cat-of-nine-tails?

CHAPTER 8
Fall 1777-Fall 1778

M r. Richards paced the cabin floor. He stuck his head out the door—probably to call the mate with the whip. He turned to face us and shook his head in annoyance. "I'll ignore the fighting between you two this time. But be careful, Chris, or I'll return you to the prison ship. And Stone, follow orders, or you'll be taking a long swim in the ocean."

The lad from Yorkshire obeyed me for a month. Most likely, he didn't want another taste of my fist.

Unfortunately, the rum must have erased Stone's memory of our battle. One day he and I were working in the cook's room. I saw that Stone didn't clean the knives and forks in a proper manner.

"Look, Stone, you left food on these." I threw down the utensils in revulsion. The three sailors in the room stopped their conversation.

Stone glared at me and his long eyebrow lowered over his eyes. "You Yankee." He picked up a table fork and stabbed me in the chest.

Shocked, I looked down. The fork had been thrust near my heart. Blood seeped through my shirt and ran freely down my clothes.

One of the sailors pulled the fork from my chest and held up the red-tipped utensil. He waved it in Stone's face. "You hog!"

Another seaman boxed Stone's ear. "You're nothing but a common brute. Davy, help me haul this boy to the quarter deck. We'll teach him a lesson."

At the sailor's insistence, I told the boatswain's mate my story of the attack. My bloody shirt was evidence of my claim. The mate immediately tied Stone to a cannon. The seaman grinned viciously at Stone. "This lad will get a dozen lashes from my cat-of-nine-tails." The mate twirled the whip in the air as the boy struggled in protest. "Please, Chris, forgive me," cried Stone. "It was a foolish mistake I made."

At the first lash, Stone screamed in pain. Blood ran down the boy's back.

The lashing and the shrieks of the young man made me sick to my stomach. Stone deserved punishment, but this was torture. Unwilling to see Stone suffer any longer, I pleaded for him. "One lash is enough. A dozen is too much for the crime."

Ignoring my plea, the mate raised his whip.

I placed myself between the mate and Stone. "That's enough!" I cried.

The mate paused, reluctant to stop. Then he grimaced. "All right. I believe the boy will mind his manners in the future."

After the whipping, Stone and I had no more fights. He was quicker to respond to my commands, and I was slower to criticize. The scar on my chest left by the fork attack reminded me to keep a distance from Stone.

After another capture of an American vessel, I met one of the lads who came on board as a cabin boy. Dark-haired John Sawyer was born on Long Island in the state of New York. He was good-humored and honest, a far cry from Stone. I asked him, "How long did you sail before you were captured? Did you get any prizes?"

"We overcame a British schooner not far from Boston. I was given my share: six pounds of sugar and five pounds of coffee." John gave a long, deep sigh. "But I lost my earnings when we were captured."

I said, "Our cruise was a failure. We had two chances, but the captain let both ships slip away."

Which is worse, I wondered? To win and then lose your prize, or never have a prize? I could understand how painful it would be to have your winnings taken from you. But for myself, I think I'd have enjoyed a few hours celebrating my share of a reward.

I spoke in confidence to my new friend. "I've been on board this ship for a few months but haven't had an opportunity to escape. The first time I get the chance, I'll be gone with the wind."

John nodded. "I'm with you."

During stolen moments, John Sawyer and I played games on the ship. One of us would hide while the other hunted for his prey. I felt light-hearted for the first time since I had been captured. Our fun reminded me of the adventures I'd had with my friend Josiah.

In October of 1777, we passed by a British brigantine in a light fog. Once we were in hailing range, the captain questioned his fellow commander. "What do you hear from New York?"

The officer responded in a heavy voice. "Unpleasant news. Burgoyne and his whole army surrendered near Albany."

I was on the quarterdeck when I heard the report. Thrilled, I ran fore and aft on the gun deck shouting the news. A midshipman swore at me. "You and your infernal lies. There are not enough Yankees on the whole continent to take Burgoyne. He has ten thousand of the best troops of Lord Howe's army."

The following day we fell in with another ship that confirmed the news of Burgoyne's defeat. I raced to the main deck to ask the crew: "Now what do you think of your great Burgoyne?"

Several voices cried, "You Yankee, be off!" One sailor called me a forbidden curse word that usually led to severe punishment. No one complained of the seaman's language, as I'm certain the British crew agreed with him.

John Sawyer took me aside. "Chris, quit bragging about America's win to our enemy. One of those sailors is going to toss you overboard."

I laughed. "I guess you're right. But maybe the Americans will win this war after all."

The *Maidstone* cruised along the edges of America, looking for prizes. We headed south near the coast of Virginia, where the captain captured several red cedar pilot boats laden with valuable tobacco. After the American crews were removed, their crafts were sunk or burned. Again and again, I saw the ships of my country destroyed. The sight made me nauseous.

The unhappy American prisoners were forced to come on

board the *Maidstone* and serve with our crew. I talked to the young men and boys who were captured. "Do you have any news of Rhode Island?" I asked them. "Are any of you from New England?" The defeated sailors shook their heads. All the prisoners hailed from Southern states.

The crew's prize money was quickly spent according to the sailors' creed: "What I had I got, what I spent I saved, and what I kept I lost."

The British crew always shared their payment with the cabin boys. Officer Richards kept my earnings of several guineas under lock and key. I wasn't sure I wanted the money taken from fallen American ships—I felt my reward was cursed.

IN LATE MARCH, we cruised to the northern states. The *Maidstone* seldom came to anchor or lay at a wharf. A few miles from my homeland, however, a group of sailors, a few boys, and I were ordered to set ashore. The location was a small island in Narragansett Bay between Connecticut and Rhode Island. Although the air was nose-freezing cold, a pale sun peeked from the clouds. Here was my chance to escape!

Mr. Richards gave us our instructions. "Gather a pile of twigs. We need to make brooms." He ordered the man in charge of the boat, "Keep a sharp lookout on my cabin boy."

When our boat reached the island, I stared at the mainland shore of Rhode Island with its familiar sharp rocks and grayish-green bushes. The land pulled at me like a mother bear gathering its cubs. Once our crew set foot on the island, I looked for a chance to escape. The mainland was about two miles away. I smelled freedom in the air.

The foul-smelling man in charge kept close to me, his eyes following my every movement. When a crew member called his attention, I seized my opportunity and raced to the water's edge. I tore off my coat and shoes and threw them down. Before I could jump in the water, a rough hand tossed me to the ground.

"I'll tell the captain to tie you up next time we're near land." The man cackled and pushed me into the mud.

My face was buried in the mud, along with my hopes of escape.

That evening, John Sawyer shook his head when he heard my tale. "You would have died trying to reach land. The water was near freezing."

"You might be right." I must admit the offensive sailor likely saved my life.

March 1778

THE *MAIDSTONE* WAS LYING near Newport Harbor when we received orders to take a ship. In all haste, we made sail for Point Judith, located on the southern tip of Rhode Island.

Mr. Richards found me cleaning his cabin. "We'll be attacking a ship from your home. It's the *Columbus,* out of Providence. Do you know her?"

"Of course, I watched her many a day." My stomach sank. She was also the ship commanded by Commander Whipple. It was possible Josiah was on board.

The officer laid his hand on my shoulder. "Stay in my cabin while we destroy the vessel. You needn't watch."

"Aye, aye." If only I could save this Rhode Island ship. Fearing what would happen to the vessel and its men, I ignored Mr. Richards and watched the attack from on deck.

The crew of the *Columbus* must have seen our vessel approach, for they ran their ship ashore at Point Judith. Their crew disembarked and drew a six-pound carriage gun up a hill. Surely, Josiah and Commander Whipple had escaped capture along with the rest of the men.

In the meantime, we sailed near the American ship and dropped anchor. Pop! Crack! From land, the crew of the *Columbus* fired their muskets and cannon at us. One of the shots sprang a leak in our hull. A musket ball whistled over my head, so I crouched to avoid being hit. Our ship fired onshore at the attackers and dispersed the men.

Captain Gardner waved his arm. "Destroy their vessel!" Our crew members jumped into a small boat and soon boarded the ship from Rhode Island. When our seamen set fire to the *Columbus*, I covered my eyes. How could I watch that fine Providence vessel sink to its watery grave? The pain in my chest was almost unbearable.

The sailors from the *Columbus* ran down the hill and fired their weapons at our small boat. After the shots, our small vessel slowly returned to the British *Maidstone*. We saw five of our men lying wounded inside the boat. Drenched in bright red blood, our crew members appeared to be dead. Captain Gardner was distraught at the sight. Then from inside the boat, an arm moved, and another man groaned. Although in bad condition, the five sailors were still alive. None died from their wounds.

I had to get away from this British ship. What kind of Patriot was I to helplessly watch over the destruction of American ships?

John Sawyer sought me out. "Here, have a cup of grog. You need something to drink." He handed me a mug. "That ship was from Rhode Island, right?" he asked.

"The British destroyed that beautiful vessel. It was a horrible sight." I turned away to hide my tears. I prayed that the Commander and Josiah were still safe.

———————

MR. RICHARDS often praised my work. "You must be pleased to be on our ship. You're receiving a share of the prizes. Besides, Britain will soon end this skirmish with your poorly armed soldiers."

I didn't answer. In my heart, I knew Britain would lose.

Mr. Richards put his hand on my shoulder. "Chris, I've been watching you with the other boys and the men on our ship. You show the ability to lead. Perhaps one day you'll be an officer in the British navy."

I wanted to tell him, "I'll always remain true to Rhode Island and my country. As soon as I get a chance, I'll escape from your ship." But I knew better than to let him know my thoughts. Instead, I answered, "Yes, sir, we'll see what fate brings."

Mr. Richards mustn't realize I wanted to escape with every

fiber of my body. If he did, he would keep an extra close watch on my movements.

I TURNED age fourteen in June. I couldn't believe I had spent almost a year on board a British ship. How were my father and my family doing? Were they well? I had no idea.

During the fall, the *Maidstone* took several prizes. Our captain ordered Mr. Richards to take one of these ships, a captured French schooner, into New York harbor. I accompanied my master onto the ship. Several sailors were assigned to bring the schooner into port. However, a sickness spread among the men and caused many to be too weak to do their tasks.

The pilot shook his head in desperation. "Chris, do you know anything about sailing?"

"Yes, I know all about it." My voyage on the privateer gave me experience.

"Then get to work."

For several days, I enjoyed scrambling up the rigging and setting the sails. The fresh air blew through my hair and cleared the cobwebs from my brain.

As we neared the harbor, the pilot handed me a guinea. "Here's for your help, son."

We arrived at the port of New York and waited for the *Maidstone* to join us. The harbor was bustling with ships and boats. Onshore, the British soldiers in their bright red uniforms were everywhere.

I was permitted to go ashore with Mr. Richards and his

mates. I felt like kissing the ground when I stepped foot on American soil. It was overwhelming to walk among the crowds of strangers after being with the same crew for so many months. I breathed in the town's smells.

While in the city, I searched for an opening to run away, but my movements were closely watched by Mr. Richards.

On our third day at the port, Mr. Richards ordered me to go ashore without him. "Take my clothing to a washerwoman in the city. You'll return them clean to the frigate by five o'clock."

At last! This was my opportunity to escape.

CHAPTER 9
Fall 1778

An English boy from London, a servant to the boatswain, joined me as I went ashore. My companion was William Rock, a tall young man with dark hair that stood on end. After we arrived in the city, we both left our bags of dirty clothes with the washerwoman. The two of us proceeded to walk about the New York City wharf.

Rock grinned. "I like this British port." Although a hardworking boy, he wasn't too clever.

"What are you saying? This is an American port. The British soldiers may control it for now, but we Patriots will regain our land."

Rock scanned the streets with care. "Where are the beasts? Are they outside of the city? I have heard tales of dangerous wild animals roaming about America."

"America is civilized. We have cities and colleges throughout the land."

"Hmm." I could see that Rock was not convinced.

"There is something you should know," I told him. "I won't be returning to the *Maidstone* with you. I plan to escape."

"Won't the beasts tear you to pieces once you leave the city?"

"No, Rock, my route to Rhode Island is safe from wild creatures. Although I will be in danger from blood-thirsty redcoats and Tories."

"Then I'll escape with you." Rock's face was aglow at this idea.

"No, don't be foolish. You're British-born, while I have family and friends here. And I support the cause of American independence."

"I think it would be a great adventure." Delighted, Rock ran his fingers through his wild hair.

"It's hazardous for me to escape, but I consider it my duty."

"I'd like to join you," said my companion.

I sensed that Rock was indeed rock-headed. "You would be severely punished if caught."

"I've decided. I'll go with you, even if it is to the end of the world."

"Come with me if you must." I wagged my finger in front of his nose. "But you are to act promptly under my direction."

Rock's face beamed with excitement. "I promise I'll follow your orders."

I had a dollar, along with the guinea given to me by the pilot. Rock also had a dollar with him. It would be enough money for our escape. The rest of my prize money, a total of 15 guineas, was kept by Mr. Richards. The extra money would be useful, but I wasn't sure I wanted the tainted money.

We didn't reboard the frigate at five o'clock as requested. We were officially on the run.

That evening, we needed a place to sleep unseen. Rock and I found an old dismantled vessel not far from Fly Market. We slept in shot lockers, I in the starboard locker, and Rock in the larboard one. The locker was damp and smelled of rotten fish, but my heart sang with pleasure. It was my first night in America in fifteen months.

At dawn, we arose and headed for the steps near the market. I warned Rock, "Make sure not to draw attention to ourselves. Since we didn't return last night, Mr. Richards may have mates looking for us today."

We found a boat unloading its cargo of milk and supplies. "May we go with you to Brooklyn when you are finished?" I asked the boatman. The man and I decided on a price. "Come back in an hour," said the man.

We kept away from the port where Mr. Richards had previously landed. We bought some bread from a vendor.

"Halt! You two, stop!" Two soldiers ran down the narrow pathway toward us.

Were the soldiers after us? I could jump into the bay and escape among the boats, but the soldiers might fire at me. I'd be better off trying to lie my way out of trouble.

"Halt!" The soldiers ran past us. They were chasing two other youths who were dashing up an alley.

My rapidly pumping heart slowed. "Whew." I pushed Rock toward the milkboat. It was time to leave. Rock and I were ready to step on board when I saw John Sawyer, my fellow cabin boy from the ship.

"Sawyer!" I hailed my friend. "The boat is leaving."

"Aye, aye." Upon seeing me, John understood at once—a runaway was in progress. Casting his bottle of milk aside, he joined us in the milkboat. I was delighted to have my friend John join us. Once on board, John put a finger to his lips and pointed with his chin to the shore. Unbelievably, there was Mr.

Richards! He was talking to a vendor only a few feet from where I'd been standing. If he saw us, he'd send soldiers after me, so I hunched over and lowered my head. John also turned away from Mr. Richards' view.

Minutes passed before my heartbeat returned to normal speed. Without any problem, we three runaways crossed over to Brooklyn in the milkboat. Not wanting to alert the pilot of our plan, we said nothing about our escape during the journey. Once clear of the boat, we three walked several miles at a rapid pace. The farther I was from the *Maidstone,* the faster thumped my heartbeat. I was a red fox, free of its cage. At last, we began to converse about our adventures.

"I left the frigate this morning under direction to purchase milk at the market," John told us. "You caused a commotion last evening."

"What happened?" I asked.

"Richards noticed your absence. He called for you several times and asked Stephen Stone if he'd seen you. Naturally, Stone had not. One of the sailors told the officer you had gone to see your mother. Mr. Richards was furious at this story and made rude comments to the man. This morning Richards came to find you. On our boat, he told me, 'I suppose Chris got lost in the city. I will likely see him in the market.' If you can believe it, Richards was only a few feet away when you hailed me. The officer almost saw you."

I did feel guilty in leaving Mr. Richards, as he had been a fair master. But my desire to be home far outweighed any allegiance to a British officer.

"I'm hungry and tired." Rock frowned and rubbed his stomach.

"Let's eat at a small house off the road," said John.

I shook my head. "No, I disagree. People will suspect we are hiding. Instead, let's eat breakfast at a tavern in plain sight. We'll invent a story to explain our actions."

Our plan was to walk almost 100 miles across Long Island to Sag Harbor, which was a port at the eastern end of the island. From there, I would sail to Connecticut and then walk home to Rhode Island. The British governed the area of Long Island and were supported by their Tory friends. We needed to protect ourselves against capture.

After a filling meal, I spoke quietly to my friends. "If we are stopped on our journey, we'll say we've just returned from catching Yankees on a privateer. We're traveling to Sag Harbor to visit our relatives and friends."

"That part is the truth," said Sawyer. "I have an uncle residing there by the name of Captain Daniel Havens. My married sister also lives in Sag Harbor, and my father is not far from there."

Our story agreed upon, we ate breakfast at the nearby tavern. We then continued on the main road to Sag Harbor. I welcomed our walk through the peaceful green country around me, a wonderful change from the grimy city.

"Stop! What was that noise?" asked Rock. He looked frantically toward the trees along the road.

"Hide. It must be a wild beast." As a joke, I pretended to be afraid.

"Ahhh!" Rock fell to the ground and huddled like a child.

"It's only a squirrel in the bushes." I laughed and pounded Rock on his back. "Don't worry, we will protect you from the wild American beasts."

For the next several miles, John and I teased Rock about his irrational fears.

On the second day of our journey, we encountered British soldiers wearing lobster-red uniforms. I showed an air of confidence, although I shivered inside. Rock, John, and I ignored the soldiers while we pretended to chat, but the men stopped us. The tallest one nudged me with his gun, saying, "Who are you, lad? No doubt you three are runaways from his Majesty's navy."

"No, not runaways. No indeed, sir." I told them our invented story, and we were allowed to proceed. Out of hearing of the soldiers, I spoke to my friends. "What did I tell you? We looked innocent, and the soldiers were fooled." My head swelled. We boys had misled the British.

The following day we were again stopped, this time by three men traveling toward New York City. These fellows, apparently Tories, led ten horses destined for market. The men examined each of us separately. I had faith in John Sawyer but worried that Rock would get confused and reveal our identity. The men, to my relief, found no discrepancies in our stories.

"So, we are free to go?" I asked.

"No. You three are certainly runaways from a British man-of-war." Their leader, a man with smallpox scars on his face, blocked our route. "We can get forty dollars per head for you boys. That will help us buy another horse."

Taking my companions to the side, I said in a loud whisper, "We'll accompany these men to New York. Then our officers will oblige these men to return us here at their own expense." The three men overheard me, as was my intention. I walked up to the best horse in the group. "I'll take this horse."

"Stand back," said the leader of the party. "I don't know what to make of you." The man pointed to Rock. "That fellow I could swear is an English boy, but you two seem to know men at Sag Harbor. One of you says that Captain Havens is your uncle." The scarred man paused, weighing the situation. He snorted in disgust. "Since I know Havens, I must let you go on."

Once we were a distance from the men, Sawyer slapped me on the back. "Hawkins, you can tell a fine story at a moment's notice." We yelped in delight, overjoyed at our success.

Without any further interruption from the Tories or the British, we arrived that afternoon at the house of Captain Havens in Sag Harbor. John explained that his uncle was a secret Patriot who hid his beliefs from the British and the Tories around him.

An attractive, dark-haired young woman dressed in blue opened the door. "John! Thank God, you're safe." She kissed our friend on the cheek. "I'll fetch Uncle Daniel."

"Great glory, who was that?" Rock's eyes nearly popped from his head.

"My cousin Sarah. She stays here while her father fights in the army," said John.

"You're lucky to get a kiss from that one," said Rock, his lips smacking.

Captain Havens, a sturdy man, came to the door. "Come in, come in, boys. I can't believe you have escaped from the British. I'll hear your tale while we eat." The captain led us to the dining area. After a short wait, he entertained us with what was likely the best food and drink his house could afford. We devoured the beef stew, potatoes, and cornbread served to us.

"You're welcome to stay here until you have a chance to

cross the Long Island Sound to Connecticut." The dark-haired man stroked his beard. "But be advised to keep out of sight as much as possible. Mind you, there are British officers on our streets in disguise."

John said, "I hope to visit my sister tonight. She lives two miles from here." Rock and I decided to go with him.

The captain looked concerned and reflected for a moment. "Very well, but conduct yourselves with utmost caution. If you are found out, I'll be accused of harboring fugitives."

We traveled with care and spent the night with John's sister and her husband. They served us a hearty breakfast of corn mush and buttered bread. In the afternoon, we three returned to the house of Captain Havens. The gentleman sat with us to hear more of our stories. He was greatly entertained by the telling of our sea and land adventures. "To think you escaped both British soldiers and Tories."

Before heading for his father's home on the island, John bid his farewell to us. "Chris and Rock, thank you for saving me from the British. I will treasure my freedom."

I was sorry to take leave of Sawyer, as he was a fine friend.

Following directions from our host, in the early evening Rock and I boarded a small vessel bound for Saybrook Point. We arrived in Connecticut at one o'clock the next morning. Once on land, we found a tavern and fell exhausted into our beds.

Rock arose at first daylight and left the room. I stayed in my bed until the sun rose higher. After breakfast, I asked the landlord, "Have you seen my companion? A tall boy with wild, dark hair?"

"I haven't seen him since he left here an hour ago."

Outside, I looked up and down the street. A roll of drums caught my attention. To my horror, I saw Rock marching with a recruiting party led by a British sergeant.

I walked alongside him. "Rock, what are you doing?" I grabbed him by his shoulder.

"I enlisted." Rock's face was beaming.

"Let me get you free." I begged the sergeant to release Rock but without success. I watched as my fellow escapee marched out of view. The young man had changed from my friend into my enemy.

Continuing my journey alone, I boarded a sloop to Norwich and arrived there late the next day. I traveled the road on my way to North Providence. The cold November weather made me shiver, but thoughts of home kept me going. I wondered if Father was there or away with the army. My anger toward him had faded. I now understood that he wanted to protect me from the war. But I shuddered to think at how furious he would be with me. First, I had run away from my apprenticeship in violation of a contract. After that, I was in service for 18 months to the British navy, our true enemy.

I held back tears as I walked on the path leading to my family home. I threw open the door.

"Christopher!" Eight small bodies threw themselves at me. I was covered with sticky fingers and wet kisses. Silas, the littlest one, hugged me around my ankles. During my absence of a year and a half, all of the children had grown like wild grass.

"Son, you're home safe." My mother was crying. She waited until my brothers and sisters moved away until she gave me a big hug.

Stephen scowled at me. "You ran away! And you never

came to say goodbye." Although taller, he was still a serious little man.

"I'm sorry, but I couldn't come home to say farewell. Father would never have approved of my decision to leave the tannery." I glanced at my mother. She was biting her lip.

Mary said, "Father is not here. He's in the army." My sister, thirteen years old, was no longer a little girl. Instead of two braids, she wore one long black braid down her back.

"How is everyone doing?" I asked.

Silence greeted me. At last, Ma said, "Times are not easy. General Washington has no money to give wages to his soldiers."

I grasped my mother's hand. "I enlisted on the privateer because I intended to share in a prize. I wanted to give you money, Ma."

"Your plans didn't work out, but sometimes life is that way." She stroked my hair. "I'm thankful you didn't drown at sea."

"You think too much about yourself, Christopher, without regard for your family or others." Mary's nose widened in anger. "What about your apprenticeship? Will you be arrested? You had a legal contract with Mr. Mason."

"I'll visit the man tomorrow. But I'm not returning to the tanyard. I'll have no more of those horrid smells." The little ones laughed as I held my nose and made a face.

That night I shared a bed with two of my brothers. They had grown, so there was less room for me. Nonetheless, I was content to be at home. My family surrounded me like a warm blanket in the November chill. But would I be forced to return to the tanyard? I didn't want to escape from one prison into another.

CHAPTER 10
December 1778

"Mr. Mason, I hope you're in good health." I sat in the parlor of my former master. Sweaty hands left dark spots on my pants. Even inside the house, the odors of the tanyard made me as ill as if I'd drunk a jug of rum.

"You did not leave in the best of circumstances, young man." With eyebrows lowered, Mr. Mason glared at me.

I used my most courteous manner with the man. "I apologize for my sudden departure. I left to be an American Patriot and to earn money for my family. Unfortunately, I didn't succeed in my venture."

The man's jaw tightened. "You know I could send you to prison. You broke a signed contract."

I bit the inside of my cheek. "Yes, you have that right. Though I do hope you'll forgive me."

Mr. Mason regarded me for several moments. "You're a bright young man and always worked hard. I'll allow you to continue your apprenticeship with me."

I shook my head. "It's not my desire to be a tanner. I'd like to return to farming. That kind of work pleases me."

"Truly?" The stern man grunted. "Then you expect me to cancel your indentures of apprenticeship?"

"I'd be incredibly grateful if you did so."

The man paced in front of me, his eyebrows fighting each other in the middle of his forehead. My nerves stretched to the breaking point. After a few moments, the man spoke. "All right, I'll terminate your contract. I don't want someone at my tanyard who is not content. You'd most likely run away again."

Relief swept through me. This man of God was treating me in a most humane way.

Mr. Mason said, "Come by next week. I'll have the papers ready to sign."

I asked farmers in the area to see if they needed a laborer. Mr. Obadiah Olney, who lived northwest of us in the town of Smithfield, consented to hire me. The older man and his son owned a large farm. The day after Christmas, I left home to reside with the Olney family.

Before my departure, my brothers and sisters gave me hugs and kisses. Stephen punched my arm.

"Don't go to sea without warning us first," my brother told me.

I hugged my mother. "Ma, I won't be far away. I'll be nearby until Father returns to stay."

At least there would be one less mouth to feed at home. Also, I intended to give my mother any extra food the farmer gave me.

I was content with my labors at the Olney farm. In the winter we repaired the equipment and tended the animals. Mistress Olney was a kindly and worthy woman, who treated me well. The farmer's daughter, Mamie, and his son's wife teased me as if I were a younger brother.

"Look at Christopher," said the daughter-in-law. "His hair

goes in five directions. He would break a comb if he ever used one."

"And the way he eats!" Mamie, a few years older than me, laughed. "He consumes enough for two workers. He should weigh 200 pounds!"

"You ladies are too kind. Always a compliment for me," I said, teasing them in return.

During winter afternoons, the ladies sewed fine needlework with exquisite details and delicate colors. They sold some of their finer pieces to wealthy women in Providence. Dorcas, their neighbor, often joined in the quilting. The young woman had curly blonde hair that often escaped her cap. At times we'd gather near the fire, and I'd tell them of my adventures.

One afternoon, Dorcas said, "Christopher, you took so many chances. I believe you were lucky to escape the British." She shook her head, causing her curls to bounce.

Mamie asked, "Christopher, what happened to the boys you escaped with?"

"John Sawyer returned to his father's home near Sag Harbor, and Rock enlisted in the British army. I've had no further news from them."

"I'd like to meet John Sawyer one day." Mamie was of the age to marry. I wondered if she thought John was a possible match.

I turned to their neighbor. "I know your family name is Whipple," I said to Dorcas. "Are you related to Commodore Abraham Whipple?"

"He and I share the same great-great grandfather, Captain John Whipple. Although the commodore is a distant relation, I consider him family."

I sighed. "I wish I'd been on Commodore Whipple's ship. Then I wouldn't have been captured."

Mamie lifted an eyebrow. "You were too young when you ran away. But I still admire you for your patriotism."

"United we will succeed against the British," I said.

Dorcas put her hands on her hips. "If I were a man, I'd join George Washington's army."

The others laughed at her unusual ideas. I winked at Dorcas. "And you'd be riding on Yankee Doodle's pony, no doubt." She blushed at my teasing.

CHAPTER 11

1779

Spring arrived, and delicate violets appeared in the woods. I labored long hours fertilizing and planting the fields along with two other young men. Although I enjoyed seeing the results of my work, I had not forgotten life at sea. During my dreams, I sometimes found myself sailing on a ship and swaying with the rhythm of the waves.

One warm and humid summer evening, there was a knock at the door of the Olneys. The farmer said, "Christopher, there's a man who says he knows you."

In the doorway was Josiah, my dear friend. He had the strength and the height of a man. His blonde hair was even lighter than before, bleached by the sun and salt air.

"Josiah, what are you doing here?" I pounded my friend on his back.

"I'm on leave. If I may sit for a few moments, I'll tell you about my adventures."

I introduced Josiah to the Olney family. Mamie's eyes lit up, bright enough to illuminate the house. Josiah leaned over to examine the young lady's handiwork. "Look at that lovely quilt you're making. I've never seen finer." Later, as we ate supper,

Josiah commented, "Mistress Olney, your pastry is sent from heaven." As usual, Josiah charmed the womenfolk.

After supper, we all listened to Josiah's stories. "Did you hear of the prizes that Commodore Whipple captured?" asked Josiah.

"Only rumors. Tell us what happened," I said.

"Commodore Whipple led the *Providence* and two other Yankee ships to Newfoundland in search of British vessels. On July 18th, we captured eleven prizes in one single day!"

The women listened wide-eyed to my friend's stories. "You and your captain are incredible," said Mamie, her face melting in adoration. "Did the ships bear precious cargo?"

"The vessels carried cotton, wines, sugar, and more," said Josiah. "I have received my share of the prize. I gave my uncle some of the coffee I earned. And look what I've brought for you ladies." Josiah spread a half-dozen lemons on the table.

"Ooh." The women touched and smelled the lemons in appreciation.

"Commodore Whipple is my relative," said Dorcas with a tilt of her head.

Josiah smiled. "Is that so? Then I'm doubly honored to meet you."

IT WAS harvest time at the farm, with chilly mornings and brisk days. Once a week, I carried a bushel of vegetables home to my mother and siblings. I gave my family every penny of the small wage I earned. While he awaited another cruise with Commodore Whipple, Josiah often visited the Olney farm.

In November, Josiah came by the Olneys to bid farewell. His second tour with Commodore Whipple was ready to begin. None of the women had a dry eye as they said their goodbyes.

With Mr. Olney's permission, Josiah and I visited my family. "Josiah!" cried the little ones as they crowded around my friend. I could have been a wooden pole for the little attention they paid me.

Josiah and I handed my mother the vegetables and ham from Farmer Olney.

"Your master is a kind soul, son." My mother placed the ham on the table. "Josiah, you are soon to leave, I imagine."

"Yes. I'm hoping to capture another dozen British merchant ships. And how is Mr. Hawkins faring in the army?" asked Josiah.

"We've not heard word for three months. But I assume that no news means all is well." My mother was thinner than ever. I always felt guilty that my family had little food while I was fed well at the Olney farm.

"My goodness, Mary, you are a young woman now." Josiah nodded his head in approval.

My sister blushed at the compliment. Under Mary's white cap, her long black hair streamed in waves down her back. I realized that Josiah was right. Mary was becoming a woman. My sister, always mature beyond her years, helped my mother raise the small ones.

My sister pressed something into Josiah's hand. "This is to remember where you came from."

Josiah opened his hand. In his palm was a small shell from the rocky beaches of Rhode Island. He smiled at Mary. "I won't forget my home. The shell will also be a memory of the person who gave it to me."

Everyone in the family gave Josiah a farewell hug. Josiah picked up young Silas and tossed him in the air. The boy screamed in delight. Josiah looked at us for a few moments. "I never had a mother or brothers or sisters. You've always been my family."

When we parted, I prayed that I would soon see Josiah again soon.

CHAPTER 12

1779-1780

During our harsh winter, I thought of Josiah often. I pictured him straining against biting winds as he sailed through rough seas. On an errand to Providence, I stopped by the house of Josiah's uncle, Captain Greene. Looking half asleep, the big man with a face like leather opened the door for me to enter. The air inside was only a bit warmer than the bitter cold outside.

"Good morning, Captain Greene. I was wondering if you have you received a letter from Josiah. It's been three months now."

The captain groaned as he leaned over to place logs on his nearly extinguished fire. "No, I fear not. But I've heard his ship is down south patrolling the Carolina coast."

"People say the war is almost over." I set a pot of water to boil over the fire for the captain. "I expect we'll see Josiah home within the month."

"They write that foolish hogwash in the papers. There's no money or supplies for our poor soldiers. This blasted cold helps the British batter us down."

"We'll never stop fighting until we win." When Josiah's uncle didn't answer, I left without another word.

Captain Greene planted a seed of fear inside me that grew into a giant weed. I'd always thought we'd beat the British. But if we failed, all those lost lives were for naught. At night I sat in front of the fire with my head down. When spring arrived, the hard labor of planting kept me too tired to dwell on dark thoughts.

One day, Mr. Olney pulled me aside to talk to me. "I have learned that General Lincoln in South Carolina has fallen to the British. They say more than 5,000 soldiers, seamen, and militiamen have been taken prisoner." Mr. Olney's eyes darkened. "Commodore Whipple and his crew were some of those who surrendered. It is likely your friend Josiah is among them."

Finding it difficult to breathe, I rubbed my chest. "May I go to Providence once I've finished work? Perhaps Josiah's uncle has more news."

Farmer Olney patted me on the shoulder. "Yes, son, you may."

On my way into town, images of Josiah came to mind. We had spent many afternoons fishing and swimming during the warm months in Rhode Island. Those days were better than jewels gained in a prize. Once in Providence Harbor, I found Josiah's uncle on the deck of his sloop. A gust of wind sprayed saltwater on me.

"Captain, what have you heard of your nephew?" I asked.

"Not good. Commodore Whipple had 220 men on board the frigate *Providence*. The crew members are listed as 'Rebels against our Lord the King.'" The weathered sailor threw a fish into a bucket, then rubbed his gnarled and leathery fingers on his pant legs. "I am certain Josiah was among those men."

"But where are they sending the prisoners?"

"I don't know as yet." Captain Greene's head sagged. "I'll tell you when I get news."

The captain sent for me mid-July, a month after my 16th birthday. When I entered his home, the captain was sitting like a stone. I choked on the strong stench of rum in the air.

"Josiah is imprisoned on board the *Jersey*." The man was slurred in his speech. "He's outside of New York City in Wallabout Bay."

"No!" Horror stories about the prison ship had spread about town. The old *Jersey* was known for its unclean and disease-ridden condition. As many as a thousand prisoners were packed in the ship's hull at one time.

The captain's shoulders sank with the weight of his despair. "People say that eight dead bodies a day are removed from that ship. Twice as many men die in that horrid prison than are killed in battles on land."

I drew my arms tight around my stomach. "Is there anything to be done?"

"Commodore Whipple is sequestered in South Carolina and can do nothing. However, I sent a request to General Washington, asking him to arrange an exchange of prisoners. Commodore Whipple has brought fame to the Continental navy. Perhaps the general will do the exchange to honor Whipple."

When I told my sister Mary about Josiah's imprisonment, I thought she might burst into tears. Instead, she was as unmoving as a granite boulder. "I'll send him letters."

"I don't know if he'll receive them." I didn't want Mary to have false hope.

"Nonetheless, I shall write to Josiah."

Even if I wanted, I knew I could not keep Mary from her plan.

Two months passed with no word of Josiah. I visited Captain Greene on his sloop.

"Have you heard from General Washington?" I asked.

"His aide wrote me that no prisoner exchanges are possible." The captain took the letter from his coat, crumpled it into a ball, and threw it onto the deck. "With all of his power, why can't Washington do something?"

"Have you heard any news from the other prisoners' families?" Several men and boys from Providence were being held in the prison ship.

"In the past two weeks, three more men have died."

There must be another way. "Perhaps Josiah can escape. He's strong and clever."

Captain Greene growled a curse word. "He'd be a fool to try. A fellow captain told me of six captives who attempted escape from the *Jersey* within this past month. The men jumped into the bay but were overheard by the night watch. The guards shot four of them in the water. A fifth captive returned to the boat, but the British attacked and killed him with their bayonets. The sixth man survived by clinging to the anchor throughout the night. Luckily, he rejoined the other captives the next day without notice by the guards." The captain spat tobacco on the deck. "Even if Josiah wanted to flee, he wouldn't have the strength after months on that floating deathtrap."

I felt a black cloud grow inside me. I stopped by my home in North Providence in need of consolation.

Mary pulled me aside, out of Mother's hearing. "I shall visit Josiah."

How could Mary think of such a crazy idea? I shook her by the shoulders. "That's impossible for many, many reasons. First of all, they'll never allow you to board the prison ship."

"I'll pass on a letter to Josiah. I don't know if he received the others."

"The prison ship is several days' travel from here. Much of the journey is behind enemy lines. Do you think you can walk among the British as if you are delivering daisies?" I remembered my journey across Long Island with John Sawyer and Rock. We had narrowly missed being recaptured on more than one occasion.

"I shall walk there by myself if need be." She sealed her lips as tight as a clamshell. I hadn't seen Mary smile since we'd learned of Josiah's imprisonment.

"If so, then I'll go with you." I knew I couldn't change her mind. Besides, I was familiar—too familiar—with the path from Providence to New York City.

With all the dangers, we couldn't risk walking there. I spoke to Captain Greene.

"My sister wants to visit Josiah."

"That is ridiculous," said the seaman. "Your dear sister, I fear, is losing her mind."

"There's no stopping Mary. Here's my idea. You can take us there in your sloop."

"All the way to New York City? We'll be captured. Speak no more of this."

I disembarked from the ship. From the shore, I shouted to the captain, "I warn you, my sister doesn't heed any advice."

A week later, Captain Greene sent me a message. When I called on him, the sea-worn man said, "This is how we'll carry out your insane idea. We'll sail in my vessel until we reach Sag Harbor on Long Island. My crew and I have a delivery to make there. A friend who pretends to be a Tory will carry you by horse and cart until you reach the western shore. He will devise some way for you to go to the prison ship."

Farmer Olney permitted me to leave. My mother wept at Mary's and my plan, but she did not try to stop us. Stephen said, "I am coming with you."

My mother squeezed Stephen's shoulders. "Absolutely not. As the man of this house, you're staying here."

It was evening in early September when Mary and I joined Captain Greene on his sloop. His crew of four men nodded at us solemnly. We slipped by the British ships near Newport in the faint light of a new moon. Stopping in a leafy inlet in Connecticut, we rested and then traveled across the sound to Sag Harbor. The captain set us ashore in a well-hidden cove not far from the village.

"I'll stay here to await you. I expect your journey will take four or five days." The captain shook his head. "Why am I helping you on this devil's errand?"

"For your nephew's sake," answered Mary, her head high.

"Of course, child, of course. I only hope I've not put your lives in danger." Before we left the ship, the captain shook my hand and patted Mary on the shoulder.

The main street of Sag Harbor was filled with gentlemen, sailors, horses, and flea-bitten dogs. I wished we had time to visit John Sawyer, but we couldn't take the chance. I found the house of Captain Greene's friend, being careful not to attract the attention of the British guards.

A large, round man with thinning hair answered the door. He gave us a broad grin. "Hello, I am Mr. Wilcox, and you must be the angels of mercy. Come inside. You need to rest before we begin our journey."

Except for his servant, the man lived alone. Over dinner, he spoke of his experiences on Long Island under British rule. "Living the role of a Loyalist allows me to come and go as I please," he said with a wink.

I eyed Mr. Wilcox closely. The man must be a spy. He had every opportunity to discover facts about the enemy, then pass on the information to Captain Greene.

After a cup of tea, the man patted his stomach in satisfaction. "Tomorrow, I have a delivery to make near Wallabout Bay. You two can accompany me."

We arose early in the morning to begin our journey to the western end of Long Island. As we traveled by cart, I recognized areas where I had walked with John Sawyer and Rock. In a day and a half, we arrived at Wallabout Bay.

Mr. Wilcox pointed out the prison ship to us. "See the large ship about a mile out in the water? She was a vessel in the British navy. They dismantled her sails and rigging and closed all the gunports. The *Jersey* is now a prison ship for captured American seamen."

Mr. Wilcox knocked on the door of a broken-down house near the shore. A boy led us inside a dusty room. A large, elderly woman with stringy yellow hair sat in a battered chair. Mr. Wilcox said, "Dame Grant, these are the two we discussed.

Children, this is where I leave you. I will return for you in the early evening."

The woman coughed and took a drag from a pipe. It was the first time I'd ever seen a woman smoke. "Come along. You'll ride with me in my boat," she said in a husky voice.

There was a rowboat at a dock near the woman's house. Mary and I climbed in and sat at the bow while two boys assisted Dame Grant into the stern of the vessel. I feared the boat would sink, but it stayed a few inches above the water. The woman was as broad as her boat, sitting with her hands at rest on widespread knees. She pointed to packages of items in the boat. "We sell articles to the prisoners. To those who have money or something to exchange, of course. I am not a charity." The woman's hoarse laugh turned into a cough.

"What do you sell?" I asked.

"Tobacco, soft bread, fruit. A little of this, a little of that."

As the boys rowed the boat to the black-hulled *Jersey*, Dame Grant spoke again. "In the *Jersey's* days of glory, she carried 60 guns and sailed the seas. Now the rebels call her a floating deathtrap."

As we approached the ship, I felt overcome with a feeling of dread. It was as if the diseased vessel was reaching out to overpower us.

The Jersey Prison Ship in Wallabout Bay, New York

CHAPTER 13

1780

After we pulled next to the *Jersey*, the boys fastened our boat to the prison ship's chain. Dame Grant cupped her hands around her mouth and called, "Here it is, gentlemen. Anything you want." We watched dozens of thin and scraggly prisoners appear on deck to look at us.

The dame called to the guard at the rail in a coarse voice. "I've brought two young children to visit their relative."

"Balderdash! You know that's not allowed." The guard dismissed her with a rude gesture.

"Mayhap one of the prisoners could search for Master Greene. The children can wave to their relative. What's the harm in that?" When the guard shook his head, the dame said with a sly wink, "I think I have a lemon cake that needs eating."

The man grumbled. "What's the prisoner's full name? I'll see what I can do."

My sister spoke up. "His name is Josiah Greene, from Rhode Island. When captured, he was sailing with Commodore Whipple."

The prisoners with money descended to the foot of the accommodation ladder to select items from our boat. Dame Grant smiled at them, showing teeth as yellow as her hair.

91

"Gentlemen, what do you desire?" The frail prisoners traded coins for small paper parcels.

The prisoners without money peered at us from the rails. Many looked like living skeletons. A man dressed in rags called, "Children, give us some coin. The woman only sells to those with money."

Mary and I looked frantically among the men for Josiah. No sign.

After an hour, Dame Grant had sold most of her packages. "Children, it's time to leave. I'm finished here."

Mary grabbed the woman's large hand. "No, we can't go yet! You must stay longer."

I heard a voice shouting from above us. A prisoner was pushing his way to the side of the ship. The man's face was nearly hidden by his ragged beard. "Hullo! Are you looking for Josiah Greene?"

Mary's eyes came to life. "Yes! Have you heard news of him?"

"Bad news, I'm afraid. I was his mate on board the *Providence* under Commodore Whipple. About two weeks ago, Josiah died of yellow fever."

My chest sank, and tears ran down my cheeks. I embraced Mary; her body was as stiff as a wooden post.

"Where do they bury the prisoners?" my sister asked, her voice eerily calm.

The prisoner pointed to the shoreline. "Some bodies are thrown overboard, but guards take most of them to shore in a boat."

Dame Grant grunted in disgust. "I see it often from my house. The soldiers do none of the dirty work. They force prisoners to dig a trench and lay the bodies inside. No ceremony, except for sand thrown over the corpses."

Mary spoke with the firmness of a colonel in the army. "I want to go to the burial ground."

With a deep sigh, the dame motioned to her helpers. "Boys, row the boat over to the shore. We'll allow the little lady to look at the spot."

In a few minutes, we neared the unmarked graves of the ill-fated prisoners. As far as the eye could see, uneven mounds of dirt spread along the sandy shore.

Without the dame's permission, Mary climbed out of the boat. Her skirts fell into the water.

The woman slapped Mary's legs. "Girl, get back in! The guards won't allow it."

Armed men, posted every few yards along the shore, were standing at the grassy edge of the bank.

My sister paid no attention to the woman's pleas. I rose to accompany her.

"You stay here," hissed Dame Grant. "Your sister has a better chance on her own."

I hesitated but realized the woman was right. Mary made her way to the makeshift cemetery. With her eyes fixed only on the graves, my sister passed in front of the first guard.

"Halt! What brings you here?" The British guard gripped his weapon.

"I'm giving respects to my departed friend." Mary continued her quest.

"Stop, or I'll shoot!" When Mary ignored him, the guard raised his musket and aimed his weapon at her.

"No!" I tried to leap from the boat, but Dame Grant and the boys restrained me.

The soldier didn't shoot but kept his weapon raised.

Mary stopped in front of a freshly dug mound. Along the shore, I saw a human bone sticking up out of the sand. More bones and a bleached skull rested on the high bank.

Mary knelt on the sand and buried the letter she had brought. I saw glimmers of white as she dropped objects onto the beach. At first, I could not make out what they were. When a calico scallop caught the sunlight, I realized she'd spread a handful of Rhode Island shells onto the sand.

Finished with her task, Mary returned past the guard. Although his chin shook with anger, the soldier replaced his gun to his side.

When she reached me, Mary fell into my arms. "Let's go home," whispered my sister.

We returned to Dame Grant's house, where Mr. Wilcox awaited us. On our return to Sag Harbor, Mary wept most of the journey. I stroked her head while my heart ached. Her hair, usually perfectly combed, was tangled in knots.

Once on the shore of Sag Harbor, Mary and I pushed through bushes to the cove where Captain Greene had left us. "I don't see him." Had the captain returned to Providence? Or worse, been captured? I collapsed on the sand, and my heart felt too exhausted to beat.

With effort, I gazed to the left and saw the bow of the captain's sloop poke out from the thick bushes. "Ahoy! Captain Greene, we've returned."

The captain's head appeared. As soon as he saw Mary's face, Josiah's uncle realized what we had found. "At least now we know." The man sank to the deck and buried his head in his arms.

We journeyed through the night back to our home. At Captain Greene's request, I spent hours telling him of the many adventures Josiah and I had shared. The captain wanted to hear my memories of Josiah.

CHAPTER 14
November 1780-Summer 1781

The pace of farm life slowed with the freezing temperatures of November. I had too much spare time and wished for more work to block my constant thoughts of Josiah.

The chill in my bones never disappeared, even after my hours by the fire. At night I poked the embers in the hearth with a rod. In the burst of sparks, I saw images of myself avenging Josiah's death. I stabbed two, three, five redcoats with a sword. My tears dried as I plotted attacks on the enemy.

One morning while I fed the horses in the barn, my arms and legs itched with impatience. "Brownie, can't you eat any faster? Your oats will rot and fly away before you finish." The horse neighed in complete indifference.

"Christopher, come to the house." Farmer Olney peered past the barn door. "There's a Town Council member who wants to speak to you."

A gentleman dressed in a broadcloth jacket over a blue waistcoat stood at the door. He gave me a slight nod. "I have a court order to share with your mother. It's best if you are there while I give the news."

"Can you tell me more?" There could be no good from this man who had his nose in the air.

"I can say nothing at this time." The man's lips clamped together like an iron trap.

With Mr. Olney's permission, I accompanied the man to my family's house. Ma's smile vanished when she saw the official.

"Is it about my husband? Has he been killed?" My mother clasped her arms around herself.

The council member shook his head. "It's not that, Mistress Hawkins. The Town Council is concerned about your children. We understand how dire your situation has become. Allow me to read you the notes from our last meeting:

N. Providence Council of 11 November 1780. Hezebiah Hawkins' family is destitute and lacking necessaries of life because Hezebiah, being a Continental soldier engaged during the continuance of this war, cannot give much assistance. Hezebiah's children include Christopher, Stephen, Mary, Deborah, Luther, Isaiah, Lydia, James, and Silas. Council resolved that the overseer of the Poor bind out to an apprenticeship the older ones of said Hezebiah's children, upon the best terms for the advantage of the town and benefit of said children. The persons who agree to take them will be paid out of the Town Treasury and the ones not old enough to work shall be cared for out of the Town Treasury. Whenever Hawkins is able to pay the same, the money will be paid into the Town Treasury.

When he finished reading the document, the council

member eyed my mother over his glasses. She sank into a chair, her head in her hands.

My mother groaned. "No, no, you can't take my children."

"It's for the best, my good woman. Christopher, you shall help me with this business. I have the names of the older children who will enter an apprenticeship: Stephen, Mary, Deborah, and Luther. Christopher, you are excluded from this list since you have a position with Mr. Olney. The four youngest are to remain with their mother. The town will provide her with corn and grain, as needed."

"How can you take my children from me?" My mother was rocking back and forth in her anguish. My hands itched to throttle this man who caused her pain.

"Believe me, it is best for everyone. The children will be given a home that provides enough food. There is a family—Mistress Williams and her three young daughters—in need of shelter. We thought they might join your household. You'll soon have extra space."

My mother didn't respond to this last comment. Instead, she stood up and said, "My husband is sacrificing for our country so that the townspeople can continue in their daily lives. Is this fair? Does my family need to be punished for my husband's patriotism?"

The man turned to me, ignoring my mother's questions. "I shall return in one or two weeks with details on the apprenticeships. I expect you'll have the older children prepared for their positions."

The council member gave a final nod to my mother. "You realize that the Town Council has your children's best interest at heart." He threw back his shoulders, opened the door, and left our house.

My brothers and sisters had been listening to the news. Stephen and Mary sat grim-faced while Deborah and Luther cried quietly. The littlest ones cried, too, knowing only that something was wrong. I took my mother in my arms and held her as she wept.

Again and again, my mind searched for ways I could avoid the breakup of my family. No ideas came to me. Once my brothers and sister were settled in their apprenticeships, I visited them. Luther and Stephen were working at a farm in North Providence, not far from my family's home.

"How are you two?" I was pleased that Luther was gaining weight. His cheeks were fuller and his body sturdier.

Luther grinned at me. "The missus is a good cook. And I like the work." Then his face fell. "I worry about Ma and the little ones. I bet baby Silas misses me playing horsy with him."

"The master is kind enough." Stephen was solemn. "He scolds us no more than Father would."

"And your studies?" I asked Stephen.

My brother shook his head. "With all the farm labor, I haven't time to study." My heart squeezed tight at the pain in my brother's face. Stephen was the scholar of the family, the one who should have kept on in school.

Mary lived with a tailor and his wife in the middle of North Providence. The man's shop was small but active. My sister worked in the back with the tailor's wife.

"How are you doing, Sister?" I examined the delicate stitches of the jade-green dress Mary was making.

"I'm happy here." My sister's face was pale and unsmiling. I saw little truth in her words.

The tailor's stout wife beamed. "Your sister has a knack for sewing. She'll make a fine tailoress."

At least my sister was busy at work. Maybe one day she'd forget her sorrows. Or if not forget them, maybe she could bury her sadness, the way a squirrel buries its acorns.

———

I TURNED seventeen years of age in June. Occasionally we heard news of my father and were thankful that he was still alive and uninjured. While I worked at the Olney farm, I often thought of the war. I was of age to become a soldier in the Continental army or a sailor in the navy, yet I hesitated to join. I still contributed food to my mother's table. Although only the four children lived at home, there was barely enough for the growing boys and young Lydia.

I noticed as I grew older, Mamie gave me strange looks. Did she now consider me a suitable partner for marriage? The thought chilled me to my toes. I was a few years younger than she, and I would always think of her as an older sister.

One steaming day in July, Dorcas talked to me about the war.

"Do you think the war will ever end?" Dorcas sighed and wound one of her blonde curls around her finger. "It's been six years since the battles of Lexington and Concord."

"It's a good sign that the fight has lasted this long. The British thought they'd crush our rebellion in a few months."

"And will you rejoin the war? I know you're a Patriot."

I grimaced. "During my last experience, I was not much service to myself or my country."

"What about getting revenge for Josiah?"

I stood up without a word and left the room.

Josiah. No one around me mentioned his name anymore. Unable to sleep that night, thoughts of my friend pursued me. For months I had pushed ideas of revenge into the dark corners of my mind. However, Dorcas' comments had lit a fire to my desire to seek vengeance on the British.

On an August day that was cooler than average, I was cutting hay with a scythe. I dripped with sweat and felt warmer than the weather warranted. Perhaps I had a fever. Daniel Clark and Stephen Scott, my fellow laborers, worked alongside me. As my scythe was not in the best order, I could not keep up my end of the work. This greatly provoked me, and I threw my scythe into a scrap heap. As I left the field, Daniel asked, "Where are you going? Are you angry?"

"I'm not pleased with my scythe. I've decided to replace it with a sword and go to sea."

CHAPTER 15
Summer 1781

I had escaped once again—this time from my life as a farmer. I'd become a Patriot fighting the British and a sailor once more.

On this voyage, I was on board the *Mariamne*, a privateer that mounted sixteen carriage guns. The vessel was commanded by Captain Christopher Whipple, Esquire, a relative of Commodore Abraham Whipple. Since I was unable to sail under Abraham Whipple, this Whipple seemed a good substitute. We had sailed from Providence and stayed in Newport a few days before setting out to sea.

Salty ocean spray splashed in my eyes and stung my skin. The rocking of the vessel was like a mother's lullaby. With no effort, I fell into the ship's rhythm. I climbed up and down the riggings to see if I still had the ability. It was as easy as climbing a barn ladder. I breathed in the brisk ocean air. There was nothing that satisfied me more than the caress of a sea breeze.

At the top of the riggings, a sailor called, "Waterman, bring us water." I looked to see the bearer of this name. Waterman was a young man in his twenties with broad shoulders. He was strong but walked with a slight limp.

I climbed down the riggings. "Hello. The men called you

Waterman. Are you related to the Watermans of Rhode Island?"

The youth gave me a big smile. "I'm from Norwich in Connecticut, but I've cousins in Providence."

"I'm Christopher Hawkins of North Providence. Have you been a seaman for long?"

"No, this is my first voyage. After turning eighteen, I stayed with the Continental army for six years. I still suffer from an injury at the battle of White Plains." He patted his wounded leg.

"My father is in the army. The wages are scant, if any," I said.

"That's the reason I'm on a privateer. I hear the crew share in the prizes."

"That's the hope. Although I have yet to see a shilling after two years on a ship."

I showed William the tricks of climbing the rigging, which he learned quickly. His injured leg didn't appear to hinder him.

For the most part, I served Captain Christopher Whipple. He was about forty years of age, with a long nose and a high forehead. Captain Whipple was a kind man and a true gentleman. I heard from his crew that he was patriotic, vigilant, and persevering. Unfortunately, two of the captain's previous ships were seized by the British. I hoped that Captain Whipple's luck was about to change.

I brought the captain's meal to his cabin. "Sir, I've heard much about Commodore Abraham Whipple since I'm from his hometown. Is it true you're related to him?"

"Most of the Whipples in Providence are related. Abraham

and I share the same great-great grandfather: Captain John Whipple."

"That's the same connection as Dorcas Whipple."

"You know Dorcas and her family in Smithfield? We're distant cousins." He smiled. "I see you're turning red. Is Dorcas someone you know well?"

"She's friends with my employer's family."

The captain winked. "I imagine she's quite a pretty young lady."

Not desiring more discussion on this subject, I left the captain's cabin. But my ears burned with the truth of what Captain Whipple said.

At dawn on the first week of our voyage, the foggy air was thick as corn mush. The clouds cleared out once the sun rose. Spying a ship on the horizon, everyone cheered as we hoped for a prize. Waterman called, "Christopher, there ahead lies our fortune!"

A second ship appeared, dimming our excitement. As the vessels gained on us rapidly, we soon found ourselves in the company of two British frigates. There was no way to outrun these larger and faster ships. The coppered *Medea,* carrying 28 guns, drew up near us. We heard a harsh call from the British ship: "Surrender your vessel, or we will broadside you."

"Aye, aye, we surrender." Facing the superior ship, Captain Whipple had little choice.

I couldn't believe my terrible luck.

The seamen were upset at the news, some of them shouting and kicking barrels. Drained of life, I collapsed to the deck. Five days on the ocean, and I was a British captive once more. There were no prizes to give to my family. I was no benefit to my homeland, my mother, or Josiah's memory.

Our crew was taken onto one of the British frigates. Once on board, we were put between decks into the cable tier, along with more than a hundred other captured American seamen. Our fellow prisoners were the crew of the *Belisarius*, which had sailed from Boston. We were so crowded that we could neither sit nor lie down. It was hard for me to breathe due to the stench of all those unwashed men.

I looked for my friend Waterman, but no luck. Being small, I crawled back onto the cable near the bulkhead where a man of standard size could not fit. Here I stretched out to sleep. My mind and body ached with misery and despair.

Despite the grim circumstances, our imprisoned crew was full of energy. The group loudly sang patriotic songs. Some of the ditties were sarcastic and demeaning to the British. The last words of each stanza in one song were, "For America and all her sons forever will shine." While singing these words, all the prisoners united their two hundred voices to a deafening level. I learned most of the words and attempted to sing the chorus. Bullfrogs have a clearer voice than I do.

The Loyalists of the frigate's crew were not pleased. The guard frequently threatened, "Stop your bellowing, or we will fire upon you!"

The guard's warning only resulted in higher notes and more enthusiastic singing from our group of American prisoners. "We dare you to fire upon us," shouted one of the seamen. "It will be half the work for you, as many prisoners are already half-dead."

The first night was spent in this manner. Despite their repeated threats, the cowardly tyrants dared not fire upon us.

The enthusiasm of our group began to lessen on the second day. As the men awakened, it was discovered that three of the prisoners had fallen and were feared dead. Their bodies were handed up the hatchway to the British guards. The ship surgeon was able to revive them.

Only two of the prisoners were allowed to visit the upper deck at the same time. Most likely the officers of the frigate feared a group of us together. Many prisoners became so exhausted that they leaned heavily against each other.

At last, I met up with my friend Waterman from the *Mariamne* crew. I pounded him on his back. "Will, here you are. I feared the British mopped the floor with your body and threw you overboard."

"During the singing, I thought I heard the sound of a cat wailing. That must have been your voice." We both laughed.

I looked around us. "Can't we prisoners overtake the soldiers? We outnumber them."

"An excellent plan!" Waterman's face lit up. "A few of us might lose our lives. But we could also lose our lives if they send us to prison."

Waterman and I approached other men with our idea, but they ignored us or laughed in our faces.

In this dreadful situation, we were kept on board the frigate for four days. After we arrived in the port of New York, Captain Christopher Whipple was sent to a prison in the city. The rest of us were directed to the *Jersey* prison ship that rested in the bay across from New York City.

The *Jersey* prison ship. This was horrible news. I would be a prisoner on board the ship that had killed my best friend.

The guards rowed us to the dark-hulled *Jersey* not far from

Long Island shore. It had no sails or riggings. The evil ship loomed ahead of us like a black, deadly dragon. My heart was so heavy it interfered with my breathing. How could I remain on board this horrid vessel that had taken the lives of Josiah and thousands of Patriots?

I had to find a way to escape.

Interior of the Jersey Prison Ship (Library of Congress)

CHAPTER 16
August 1781

As we neared the prison ship, we saw hundreds of men on the upper deck. The emaciated prisoners were clothed in rags. Some of the men waved their hats and called out to us. Even before we boarded the prison ship, I smelled a foul vapor coming from the hull's air holes.

Once our crew was put on board the *Jersey*, we were told the total number of prisoners amounted to about 800 men. This was a ship built for only half that number. Before dark, we were ordered to go between decks for the night. The guard called, "The walking dead not yet buried, go down below." Once the hatchways were fastened down, the hold was in complete darkness. I stumbled over men as I looked for a place to rest. Perhaps I was near the spot where Josiah drew his last breath. My body shivered violently.

Throughout the night, I heard moans and curses from the ill and delirious. The intensity of the heat in the hold almost stopped my breathing.

In the early morning, I felt something pestering me. On inspection, I saw black spots of vermin on my shirt. I jumped up, brushing off the worms. Looking around, I could see vermin crawling over everyone, especially on the wretched men with the mark of death on their faces.

At eight o'clock, a guard yelled down at us. "Time to go up top, you worthless rebels!"

A prisoner responded, "We worthless rebels will defeat your feeble-brained King." As the outspoken man climbed the gangway, the guard hit him with his gun. The prisoner fell several feet down into the hold. The rest of us filed past the guard without a word.

Once on deck, I found my friend Will Waterman. We walked around the ship to breathe in the fresh air. "Isn't this place torture?" asked Waterman.

"I know far more of this ship than I wish to. Last year we came here to visit my friend, a prisoner. Too late, though, as he had died of yellow fever."

"That's a shame," said Will. I could tell by his eyes he had lost friends in the war.

A walking skeleton bumped into Waterman. Delirious, the man cried out, "Don't touch me, you beast!" Before we could walk out of the man's way, the prisoner sliced Waterman on his cheek with a hook. Other prisoners grabbed the man and wrenched the hook from his hand.

I tore a piece of my shirt to slow the blood on Will's cheek. "Are you all right?"

"I'll manage." Will pushed back his bloody hair and held the cloth to his wound.

My friend and I asked a guard for rations. He shoved us with his gun. "No food until you dullards are put into messes." After a few hours, the guards formed us into messes—groups of six men each—and finally fed us. My portion of food was a moldy, worm-filled piece of bread and a small piece of raw pork. I lost my hunger at the sight but forced myself to eat. During my meal, I witnessed a prisoner steal food from a weak man who closed his eyes for a moment.

A few feet away, shouts broke out. "You animal!" A man that looked like an animal himself attacked a fellow prisoner. To my surprise, the guards ignored the fight. I despaired that many of the prisoners had let go of their humanity. They became beasts only concerned about themselves.

A prisoner with an eerie smile stopped to talk to me. "Young man, you're new here. How are you faring?"

"I'm fine for now. But I see sick men everywhere."

The man scratched his beard, and several vermin fell to the deck. "Most of the men have dysentery—the bloody flu."

"Doesn't anyone help the ill?"

The man pointed across the bay. "See that British vessel? It's a hospital ship, but none of our men are allowed to go there. Every day, a dozen men are sick by early evening. Before morning, Death comes for them."

I remembered my sister looking for graves on the shore. "Where are the dead prisoners buried? Isn't it nearby?"

With a bony finger, the man pointed out a spot on the sandy shore. "They disturb one body to bury another. That's how many men are dying in this deathtrap."

The filth on the ship was horrifying. As there was no way to clean oneself except with saltwater, every prisoner was infested with vermin on his body and clothing. I observed a prisoner on the ship's forecastle with his shirt in his hands, having stripped it from his body. He deliberately picked the vermin from his shirt and put them into his mouth.

I approached the man. "Hullo. My name is Hawkins, from Providence. And you are?"

"I am Martin. I sailed in a privateer from Marblehead, Massachusetts."

"How long have you been a prisoner on board this ship?"

After some thought, he answered, "Two and a half years."

From lack of food, the man was nearly a skeleton. His clothes fell off him in rags, and he was all but naked. Was he truly held captive for that length of time? Perhaps due to his sufferings, he had lost track of time.

In the late afternoon, a giant of an officer gathered the prisoners and called roll. He read us the ship's regulations. "Every captive who should be detected escaping from this vessel—by swimming, taking the ship's boat, or any other way— will suffer instant death and will not be returned on board alive."

The officer's speech took the air from my lungs. There were guards everywhere. Escape seemed impossible.

Will and I talked to prisoners who had been on board the prison for a few months.

I asked a young man, "Have you thought about escaping from here?"

He shook his head. "Every day, but I want to keep alive."

"What about swimming across the bay to shore?" asked Will.

A black-bearded man pointed to dozens of soldiers standing guard on land. "See all those sentinels? They line the banks of the cove for miles."

The older man placed his bony hand on my shoulder. "You'd have to swim between two and a half to three miles to go around those guards. Besides, the water is cold enough to freeze off your privates. Are you going to survive that?"

At night I found a place to sleep on the larboard side of the ship, with my face near the wall. Two boys from Connecticut named Smith were near me. Waterman lay under a bench. Though exhausted, I couldn't fall asleep. I thought about the ship and my conversations with the prisoners. My body ached. I wondered if I had a fever.

During the night, no more than two prisoners were allowed to visit the upper deck at the same time. Only one gangway to the upper deck was open, about twenty feet from my place to sleep. Due to the bloody flu, the calls of nature were violent. The afflicted raced up the gangplank to relieve themselves. This caused a constant running over me by the sick.

I had to escape from this deathtrap, no matter the dangers.

As soon as Will awoke the next morning, our second morning on board, I told him of my intention. "I don't want to die a miserable death on this ship. Will you accompany me in an escape?"

Waterman's face flushed, and his wound reddened. Without hesitation, he answered, "Certainly."

I was pleased, as I knew Waterman was a strong swimmer. We asked others to go with us but with no success.

"Forget about your impossible idea," said a sailor with a foul, matted beard. "I've seen too many die in their attempts to escape."

A fierce-faced prisoner spat on the floor. "Don't be addle-brained."

One older man spoke in soothing tones. "We'll be released when America wins the war. There's no need to leave." Others agreed and urged us to stay. But we had already made our decision.

"Let's do this." Waterman and I clasped hands in agreement.

A man who weighed less than my sister Mary spoke. "I made plans at first, but now I'm too weak to escape. Go down to the lower deck. There you'll find unguarded gunports, your best chance for escape."

Waterman and I climbed down the steps to the next level. No guards were in sight. We saw the gunports—the openings through which cannons were fired. Iron bars were bolted across the ports to prevent escape. Will asked, "How do we break the bolts? And without attracting the guards' attention?"

"We'll find tools."

After searching the upper decks, we stole an old ax and crowbar from the cook's room. Fortunately, a thunderstorm arrived that afternoon. Under the protection of nature, we set out to break one of the gunports.

"Wait until there's thunder," I said. "Then we'll both strike against the bolts." Waterman and I waited with upheld tools. Crash! A peal of thunder roared, and we struck our ax and crowbar against the bolts. When the peal of thunder subsided, we stopped and waited. There came another roar, and so in that way we continued with our labor.

At last, we knocked the bolts and the bar loose. We slapped each other on the back in congratulations. William leaned against the ship wall, panting. "We can't leave the gunport open like this. The guards might notice." He and I replaced the bolts and bars as best we could. I grabbed some old clothes from the floor and hung them over the shattered gunports. I didn't want carelessness to spoil our plans.

The day after the storm, our third morning on board, Captain Whipple was allowed to visit his men on the prison ship. Waterman and I spoke to our captain in private.

I boldly raised my eyes to the captain's face. "Captain Whipple, Waterman and I intend to escape."

"Hawkins, what craziness!" He shook me by the shoulders. "You're bound to fail and die in the process. Only a handful of men have ever escaped from this prison ship. You are fools to attempt it."

I folded my arms. "Thank you for your advice, but we're determined to escape this evening."

The captain sighed. "What are your plans?"

I pointed in a northeastern direction. "We'll swim past the guards to a spot on the banks of Long Island. That way, we can avoid the sentinels who are stationed onshore."

"No!" Captain Whipple gasped in horror. "You intend to swim that far?"

"We must swim to a place with no guards," I answered. "There's no other way."

"Hawkins, you'll only throw your lives away. As cold as the water is, not a man on earth can swim to that point onshore. How far do you think it is?"

"We estimate the distance at a mile and a half," said Waterman.

"It's all of two and a half miles. You cannot measure across the water as well as I can. Stop your plans. I may be sent home next week. If so, it is my priority to arrange for all of my crew to be part of a prisoner exchange." The captain looked at both of

117

us, then shook his head. "I see the resolve in your eyes." He put his hand on my shoulder. "Hawkins, there is one chance in a hundred that you will get home. But if you accomplish your task, I have a request. Should you get to Providence, please visit my mother and inform her of my recent fate."

"Yes, Captain, I promise."

After the captain turned away, his comments weighed on me. Many of my decisions in life had been made without much thought. Perhaps Waterman and I were foolishly planning our deaths.

CHAPTER 17
Fall 1781

After Captain Whipple left the ship, Waterman asked, "Does the captain's warning change your mind about our escape? Perhaps Captain Whipple can arrange our release."

I snorted in disgust. "Don't believe it. I know from experience that General Washington will not approve exchanges. He couldn't save my friend."

"Should we wait for a month or two? The war could be over soon." Waterman rubbed the half-circle wound on his face. The gash was surrounded by inflamed skin.

"Let me think more on this matter." I walked away from my friend.

Alone, I paced around the ship a few times, pushing aside the men that blocked me. There were dozens of ways I could die during my escape. I could drown. Or be shot by the guards. Or be captured and killed on land. Different scenes flashed through my mind. In all of them, my face was frozen in a final death cry. I saw my mother's face, despairing at the loss of the son who had deserted her. Waterman's fate was also in my hands since he looked to me as our leader. What if I made the wrong choice?

Waterman was in the hold, rocking back and forth on a bench. I grabbed his shoulder, and he looked up at me. "Will, listen to my thoughts. Even within a week, we'll be weakened from lack of food and sleep. We won't have the energy to escape. Besides, every day the bay water turns colder. Now is our best time." I pounded the wall above Will. "I'm not dying the way my friend Josiah did."

Will's eyes opened wide, from fear or hope, I didn't know. He asked, "Do you truly think we have a chance to succeed?"

I hesitated for only a moment. "The chance of escape is small. But we have even less chance of survival if we remain on this death ship."

Will slapped his lame leg. "I'll join you. Your reasons make sense. Besides, I prefer quick suffering to long, drawn-out torment."

We each packed our clothing in the knapsacks we had made. I gathered a woolen sailor jacket, a pair of thick pantaloons, one vest, two shirts, two pairs of stockings, one pair of shoes, a pair of heavy silver shoe buckles, a pair of knee buckles, two silk handkerchiefs, and four silver dollars. I gave the remainder of my apparel to the Smith boys.

I included a bottle of rum we had purchased on board at a dear rate. Though the liquid tasted nasty, it would give us warmth and a touch of temporary courage.

My knapsack was quite heavy. Two strong straps passed over my shoulders and under each arm. The straps fastened with a string near the center of my chest. Thus equipped, Will and I were ready to commit ourselves to the water.

The time to leave was upon us. It was a mild evening for that time of year and a good night for our escape. The air was hazy, the temperature mild, and the night as dark as soot. Below us, the current flowed in a direction ideal for our swim.

Waterman and I had been on board the *Jersey* for only two nights and three days, although it seemed like an eternity in hell.

In our final preparations, we returned to the lower deck and uncovered the gunport we had broken open yesterday. As before, there were no guards in sight. We unwound a piece of rope that was stretched around a cable to use for our descent. Several of the prisoners were gathered around us. A bald man said, "Good luck, you fool-hearted knaves."

Another prisoner shook his head. "You're off to your watery graves."

Waterman and I reviewed our escape plans. I said, "We'll use the lights from the ships and the calls of the sentinels onshore to guide our course."

During the day, we had seen a house onshore along the banks. "We'll meet at the barn of the gray house," said Waterman.

"Agreed." I removed my clothing and placed it in my knapsack. "I'll swim better without my clothes dragging on me." I replaced my hat firmly on my head.

Waterman hesitated and looked down at his blood-stained shirt. "The cold water will freeze off my behind. But you're right, our clothes would only slow us." He followed my lead.

I fed the rope through the open port until it dangled above the water. Two of the prisoners held on to the other end of the rope for us. Waterman was the first to leave the ship through the gunport. Using his hands, Waterman held on to the rope until he was a foot above the water. It was agreed that at any sign of detection, we'd pull him back into the ship. Waterman let go of the rope and slid into the water with a slight splash. No shouts came from the guards. My friend was safe. At least for now.

According to our plan, I waited one minute until I followed him. After a deep breath, I grasped the rope and looked down at the black water. It would be my freedom or my grave. My hands let go of the rope, leaving the ship and my British captors behind me. The cool water both shocked and invigorated me.

I swam close to the ship's side until reaching the stern, then set out to the shore. Slowly I moved forward, my body as deep in the water as possible. I expected a gunshot from the guards to hit me at any moment. But no signs of attack, at least not yet. When I was far enough from the *Jersey* not to be noticed, I swam at a faster pace. After gaining some distance from the ship, I called, "Waterman. Waterman! Are you there, Will?" No answer.

I continued on my way. I hoped nothing bad had happened to my friend. I knew he was brave and an excellent swimmer despite his lame leg. My knapsack grew heavier with each stroke. It felt like an iron pot and a couple of boulders had been added to my load.

The light reflected by the ships' lanterns guided my course. Every half hour, the sentinels onshore called, "All's well." Their signals helped me keep track of my time in the water.

Where was my friend? I prayed we'd meet up onshore or at the barn. But an image of Will sinking to the bottom of the bay filled my head.

After swimming for nearly two hours, my knapsack broke loose from my back. I put the bag under my left arm, using only my right arm to swim. I soon discovered this led me to stray from my course. Besides, my right arm screamed with pain.

I pulled part of my vest out of my knapsack and kept the other portion of the vest still inside. Taking the vest in my teeth while throwing the knapsack over my shoulder, I again proceeded to swim. I reminded myself of the story of the sly fox Reynard, who carried a stolen goose in his mouth across the water.

I was again off my true course. The load of the knapsack cramped my neck, and the pain was almost unbearable. After swimming for more than two hours, I was now chilled inside and out from the coolness of the water. Then I saw something dark ahead of me. Land at last! But I needed to swim beyond the row of sentinels on land.

Although numb from the cold, I could still swim. However, with every stroke my bundle weighed me down more and more. I hesitated whether or not to part with my knapsack forever. At last, I sent it adrift. After the bag was gone, I felt as cool and collected as perhaps at any period of my life. Without the burden of my knapsack and contents, I set on my true course, still guided by the light from the ships. The sentinels onshore sang again, "All's well." I thought, "That is a lie, for I have tossed aside my clothing, money, and a bottle of rum, and all is *not* well."

The next sentinel's cry was faint. I had passed by all of them. With new energy, I swam for shore. It was not until I was twelve feet from land that I could touch the bottom. My feet found ground, but I couldn't stand. After so long at sea, my "land legs" had left me. I moved around in shallow water until I could stand and at last rested on the shore. Groaning from deep inside my gut, I thought about how I'd set my clothes and money adrift not more than twenty-five minutes earlier. The fish would find my shoe buckles a curiosity.

I was completely naked except for a small hat on my head. What a situation I was in! I had no covering to hide my body, I was in enemy territory, and I was without food or the means to buy food. The inhabitants of Long Island were mainly Tories, who were unrelenting. I faced perils ahead, with nothing to aid me but the help of heaven.

Yet I had succeeded in a crucial part of my adventure. I was on land after escaping the prison ship. I had swum for two and a half hours, a distance of perhaps two or three miles.

Will and I planned to meet about half a mile from here. Setting course for the house, I stumbled over a rock and fell to the ground. Angered, I gave loose to a chain of profane language. My bare skin was cut all over. I rubbed the worst bruises with my hands. The passion of anger, together with the shock of my fall, seemed to quicken the circulation of my blood. Warmth spread throughout me.

I found the gray house and its barn. After quietly opening one of the barn doors, I saw a place to lie down near a large body of hay.

"Waterman! Waterman, are you here?" I called my friend, but not so loudly as to awaken the family inside the house. Will didn't answer, and my hopes sank. Perhaps he'd found his way to a house near Hurl Gate on the Long Island shore. A fellow prisoner had spoken of this spot.

I guessed it was about three o'clock in the morning. I lay down on the floor, gathered hay to cover myself, and fell into slumber. Towards morning, I dreamt I was back on board the *Jersey*. A man with a skeleton's face and smallpox leaned over me. "Come closer, boy, breathe in my disease." I awakened, covered with sweat. I shook the images from my brain and deeply inhaled the comforting smells of a farm. The phantom of death vanished.

No more prison ship. But even though free, I had to be smart and patient to keep my liberty. I was alone, with no clothing or food. I planned to walk 100 miles across the length of Long Island to the town of Sag Harbor. From there, I'd sail to Connecticut and walk home. It was the same journey as three years ago with Rock and John Sawyer, but I was no longer a careless boy of fourteen. Impulsive acts could be my downfall.

Around nine o'clock in the morning, a black girl came into the barn. Muttering about finding the door open, she looked for eggs. I feared she could see me if she glanced in my direction. Or that she'd hear my stomach grumbling from hunger. After a while, she left the barn and shut the door.

I looked at my body, which was covered with scratches, marks, dried blood, and bruises. I must look as if I'd been in a bad fight and lost. My shoulders ached from the strain of my swim. I knew I dared not go outside during daylight in my current state of undress. I would frighten anyone I saw in my immodest condition without clothes.

I'd have to wait until night to emerge. And to give Will a chance to meet up with me.

The sun finally set. And still no sign of Waterman. When all was quiet around the house, I left my spot since I was craving food. I attempted to milk a cow in the farmyard. The cows were so afraid of my naked self that they didn't let me approach. At my touch, they'd have run like deer. Fearful the noise of the cattle would awaken the household, I headed east.

Rain began to fall in large drops, and the hard pellets stuck my naked back. My bare feet were soon blistered and bloody. I proceeded across fields and meadows, not wanting to risk travel on a road. After some time, I went through a gate into more fields. I found a melon yard and picked up two melons. I took them with me, as I needed a tool to open them.

On hearing the sounds of a horse, I feared an enemy was upon me. This part of Long Island was infested with German Hessian guards. These Germans had come to America to fight on the side of the British. On closer examination, I saw the noise was only a white horse without a rider. Or perhaps the horse was a ghost, and I was also dead. I shook my head to clear these strange thoughts.

After going some distance in the rain, I came to a fence that was made of wood and stone. I used a stone to break open a watermelon. Starving, I took a big bite but at once spit out the rotten fruit. The melons were bitten by the frost. I kept on my course and found a road and a gate. It was the same gate I had passed by before. Discouraged, I realized I had been wandering in a circle.

Setting off in the opposite direction, I traveled for a few hours through meadows and shrubs, at times going through thickets of briars that tore my naked skin. I went through a field and found corn to eat. The rain fell during most of the night, at times in torrents. The air was quite chilly, obliging me to walk fast to stay alive. I was weary to the bone. At one point, I found a spot near a fence under some shrubs. I broke off twigs and branches for cover and lay down on the boughs to rest. Despite my efforts, the rain still found me. I knew I must put myself in motion or inevitably perish.

During the night, I visited a graveyard by accident. I stumbled on a headstone, which was the first sign I was among the dead. As a result of my fall, I scratched and bruised the skin on my legs and chest. I knelt and felt the letters of the headstone inscription. I wasn't frightened by my discovery of the dead. I knew I had more to fear from the living.

CHAPTER 18
Fall 1781

Long Island

Toward daylight, I spied a barn. Inside was a wagon laden with salt hay. I found a suitable corner of the building and prepared a place to rest. The damp salt hay soon made a lively impression on my fresh briar wounds. The duration of the pain was short, however. Perhaps the hay's saline properties would help to heal my scratches.

It was almost daylight when sleep stole upon me. A few hours later, I awoke to the sound of a voice. A man was inside the barn and speaking in Dutch to himself. The farmer began unloading the hay from the wagon. I lay motionless in the hay, fearing the man would discover me.

Before the farmer finished his tasks, a neighbor visited him. The two spoke in English.

"I need to make a coffin. That fellow must be buried today," said the visitor.

Well, *this* fellow is not being buried today, for I am not yet dead.

During the men's conversation, I learned that a young man had died suddenly the evening before.

The two men left. I remained in the barn for an hour or two, then exited away from the house. As my stomach was growling with hunger, I went into an orchard behind the barn. I found and ate two half-rotten pears. Except for the distasteful melons and some raw corn, I had fasted since leaving the old *Jersey* two days earlier. I began traveling southeast along the side of a road.

After the torrents of rain, the sky was clear and the weather pleasant. I walked for an hour and saw a field of potatoes ahead of me. I intended to carry away a few of the potatoes, light a fire, and roast them. As I entered the potato patch, I saw a young woman with a basket. Unfortunately, she also saw me. I was, of course, naked except for the hat on my head. The frightened woman ran screaming and screeching toward a house.

Fearing I would be found, I ran faster than she did in the opposite direction. I traveled to a glade of trees by the side of a small bay. I went far into the woods, worried I might be pursued by Tories and their dogs. To defend against canine Loyalists, I armed myself with a heavy club. I further determined I would jump into a nearby cove if followed. After two hours, I considered I was safe from attackers.

I figured I had traveled six or seven miles since I began my travels. Keeping to the left of the cove, I soon found a bay on my right and a road on my left. I dared not travel by road. Hunger now preyed upon me, and my body was weak. I searched in vain for something to eat. I only found a few ears of corn in a field. It was not much, but it sustained me. For that day and the following night, I made no visible progress in my journey. Early in the evening, I crept into another barn and lay upon flax. This was a poor bed for a naked and hungry boy, but I slept considerably. I arose from my bed of flax at the first signs of daylight. As I resumed my same course, I walked in the fields between the bay and the road.

Along the way, I saw farmers at their labor in the fields. I decided to approach two of them, hoping they were not Tories. By this time, I was worn out with hunger. Two tall young men were gathering crops. They were astonished at my appearance and drew away from me.

I spoke to the men, trying to cover my nakedness. "Don't be afraid of me. I am only a boy."

"Are you scared?" one man asked.

"No," said I. They were the ones who appeared frightened.

The two young men advanced toward me with care. The taller one inquired, "Why are you naked?"

I slumped to the ground, too weak to stand and too tired to invent a story about my situation. I covered myself as best I could and told them the truth about my escape.

"We wish you were at home," said the young man with a birthmark on his cheek.

From this reaction, I felt they were friends.

"What do you want of us?" asked the taller one.

"I'm hungry and need some clothes. It has been three days since I had a meal. If you can help me, I pray you would."

The taller man motioned to the ridge above. "Keep down from the sight of those folks up there. Stay with my brother while I hear what my mamma says about your request."

The brother soon returned from his house. He brought me a pair of decent pantaloons, which I immediately put on.

"Go by the barn, and my mother will give you a shirt." He handed me two large pieces of buttered bread. "Keep out of sight of the farmers on the ridge," he repeated. "If they see you, they will take you to the sheriff."

I ate my food in haste. Nothing had ever tasted better to me.

Behind the barn, I found an older lady with a shirt on her arm. I could tell by her apparel that she was Dutch, as she wore a white cap with flaps over her ears.

"Son, do you have a father and mother?" The woman spoke with a Dutch accent.

"When I left home, my mother was alive. My father is in the Continental army."

The gray-haired woman nodded. "I wish you were at home with your mother now. And she wishes the same, I am sure."

The Dutch woman handed me two more pieces of well-buttered bread. "My son told me you have fasted. Careful, now, don't eat too much at one time. Your stomach won't take it."

I ate only one of my pieces of bread and stopped.

"Good," she said. She looked around the corner of the barn, then turned back to me. "You must go into the barn, take the pantaloons off, and throw them out to me. I will hang the pants and the shirt on that fence. Once I leave your sight, come out and grab the clothes. And if you are captured, you must swear you took them from the fence where they were hung out to dry. That will be no lie."

"Yes, of course. I cannot thank you enough."

"And for God's sake, don't let my servant woman see you." She pointed to a large woman who was washing on the stoop. "She will tell on me, as she is as big a devil as any of the King's folks. And then we should all be put in prison and die." Tears began to run a course down the wrinkles on her face. "Two years ago, my husband was sent to prison. He rotted and died there last month." She began to shed tears in profusion, causing tears to come to my eyes.

After a few moments, the Dutch woman dried her face. "Where are you heading?"

"Sag Harbor."

"If you travel down this road to the ferry, the people on the way are the King's folks and will certainly capture you. And if you go three and a half miles back to the tide mills, three hundred Hessians are stationed there on patrol. But if you go across the cove to the main road, that would lead you safely to your destination. Do you know how to cross the cove?"

"I'll swim across."

"No, don't try to swim. No man has ever dared to do so. You cannot do it." The woman was as fearful as if I were her son.

"I trust I can." My thoughts went to my long swim from the old *Jersey* ship to the shore.

"No, no, they say it is a mile across. You will drown. There is a canoe and an oar on the cove's bank in the bushes. These you must steal. Once across the cove, fasten the canoe on the other side, and the owner will find it. And here's a coin for you to buy food."

"Thank you. I'm greatly in your debt."

At last, we bid our farewells. I followed her directions about taking the clothes hanging on the fence. Once fully dressed, I headed to the cove. How pleasant to feel clothes on my body, rather than exposing myself to the weather and the thorny bushes. And I was delighted to avoid the embarrassment of exposing far too much of myself to others.

At the cove, I discovered the canoe and oar and quickly

crossed the water without incident. I fastened the canoe on the opposite shore as directed.

The Dutch woman had told me I was no more than nine miles from where I had started my journey. It was now two and a half days since I had left the old *Jersey*. I felt I'd suffered enough for a lifetime.

And nary a sign of Waterman. I prayed he was safe on his journey. After I crossed the cove, I traveled along the road. Whenever a suspicious character appeared on the road, I pretended to be fixing the fence on the roadside. This slowed my progress.

The sun was about an hour above the evening horizon when I came into view of the village of Jamaica. I saw sentinels guarding the town, two on either side of the road. I knew I was in great peril. I concealed myself in bushes near the roadside. What plan should I follow?

While devising ways to pass the sentinels, a black man appeared with a small drove of cattle. What if I helped the man as he passed through the village? Grabbing a stick, I hustled to the road and joined his drive, moving ever closer to the British sentinels. The black man kept his eyes on me but said nothing. Ignoring the guards, I poked and prodded at the cattle with a stick. This device had the desired effect. The sentinels did not hail or stop me.

A mile past the sentinels, I left the drove of cattle. My spirits were greatly improved. If I kept my wits about me, I'd outsmart the British. I traveled to a busy white tavern, but I dared not enter it. I decided to wait in a nearby orchard until dark. The rain began. Once all was quiet, I tried the barn but found locks on the doors. Wanting to rest and get out of the rain, I lay in a manger in a shed attached to the barn.

I must have dozed because I opened my eyes to the bright light of a lantern. A stout man was standing over me, speaking in an angry voice. "Jack, take a look. Here lies some person in the manger! He must be a scoundrel who is after our horses."

CHAPTER 19
Fall 1781

"Who the devil is it?" asked the companion, who was as thin as Jack Sprat. He looked at me distrustfully as I lay in the manger and pretended to snore.

"I don't know, he's asleep."

"Let's wake him up and see who he is."

Jack Sprat shook me, inquiring, "Who are you?"

"A friend," I answered, as if half asleep.

"Why are you here?"

I raised myself on my elbow, pretending to be in a state of intoxication. "I came in to get out of the rain."

"Where did you come from, and where are you going?" asked the stout man.

"I'm going to Jamaica." I fell back into the manger as if quite drunk.

Jack Sprat observed, "The boy is as drunk as the devil, for he can't sit up."

"A thief, I'll wager. After we put up the horses, we'll take him into the house and find out who he is."

The stout man said, "Leave the boy for now. He won't get away, as drunk as he is."

I feared questioning would get me into trouble. As soon as

the men left my sight, I scrambled out of the shed and scurried through the orchard. Once on the plains, I ran as fast as I could. It was cloudy and dark, but the rain had ceased. After traveling some distance, I came to a stop and listened for anyone who might be in pursuit. I heard no sign of danger.

When I was over the plains, I discovered a barn. Three-fourths of the barn's roof was gone, but I found a sheltered area. Making myself a bed of straw, I lay to rest. As soon as I was settled, rain fell in torrents. My slumbers continued until the sun rose, showing a clear and sunny sky. This was my fourth morning since leaving the old *Jersey*, yet I felt as if months had passed. I arose from my place of rest and traveled east on the road.

I had not progressed more than a mile before I spied a two-horse wagon accompanied by armed soldiers moving toward me. I was not pleased with the costume of the soldiers. Their red coats were a sure indication that they were soldiers of King George. I hid in the bushes until the men passed. In a short time, I discovered another wagon up ahead. I remained until twenty-two wagons, all accompanied by soldiers, passed by me.

When the road was quiet at last, I continued my travels. Seeing a fork in the road, I wasn't sure which path led to Sag Harbor. A passing boy directed me to the left road. In a few moments, I saw a house that matched the description given to me by the Dutch woman. She had instructed me to stop here. She had told me a gentleman would assist me upon hearing my story. "Hello? Is anyone home?" A lady with a narrow beak of a nose appeared.

"Is the gentleman of the house available?" I asked.

"He is not at home and not expected for several days. What is your business with him?"

I told her about my escape from the prison ship and my destitute situation. "A friend told me I could get relief by calling on you and telling my story."

The lady stepped back and sniffed in disgust. "You will get no relief from this house. How dare you presume to call on us? If my husband were at home, he would have you sent back to the prison ship."

Realizing she was a Tory, I backed away from the door.

"We are under the government of the King here," she said.

"I am sorry to disturb you." I took my leave without hesitation.

I felt the woman's eyes on me but did not look back. Instead, I ran and headed for the woods on the edge of her yard. I feared the woman would send someone to capture me. The trees scraped my face as I rushed through and stumbled on the uneven path. Did I hear dogs? Perhaps she had called a search party to capture me. After an hour, I sat to rest. I couldn't understand why the Dutch woman had sent me to the home of Tories. Perhaps I had mistaken the house. Or did the woman want me captured?

I saw the village of Oyster Bay ahead of me. This was not where I wanted to be! The boy had sent me on the wrong path. I had walked miles in the wrong direction, and I was even farther away from Sag Harbor. Now my encounter with the Tory woman made sense. Due to my misstep, I had called on the wrong house. The Dutch woman was not to blame.

My stomach rumbled, and the sky moaned with distant thunder. I couldn't stand undecided for long, as my thin clothing was not warm enough against the cold. I hesitated but decided to approach the village. Whistling as if I were merely on an errand, I walked through the streets of Oyster Bay. I could tell the British were well established in the area, as soldiers stood on every corner. I hoped my hunger hadn't made me careless. Perhaps there would have been a way to bypass the village.

When I was at the center of the village, a ragamuffin of a man came out of a grocery. He was untidy, and his British soldier jacket was unbuttoned. The unkempt man asked me, "Where are you going?"

"I'm going home if I can get there." I forced myself to sound unbothered by the question.

The man beckoned to a companion. "Go tell the sergeant to come out with a file of men."

I looked around for a place to hide, but there was no time to escape. The Tory soldiers burst out of the gray building, carrying guns and bayonets. They surrounded me as though I were a prize criminal.

I couldn't be captured, not again. I pushed myself through the soldiers around me. Instantly, a dozen arms grabbed and dragged me into the gray building. Sick to my stomach, I almost vomited.

After taking me to a room, the Tory sergeant hurled questions about where I had been and where I was going. What was my story to be? He would surely know if I told falsehoods, as I had no reasonable excuse to explain my presence in Oyster Bay. I decided to throw myself on his mercy.

I gave the sergeant a true statement, giving the history of my last voyage at sea, my capture, my escape from the old prison ship, and my subsequent sufferings. I disguised nothing. Three years earlier, in the company of Sawyer and Rock, I had successfully lied and escaped capture. But at that time, there were three of us, I was younger, and was better clad. Besides, I hoped that my true history would invite my captors' compassion rather than their hatred. But I was disappointed. The greasy-faced sergeant put on an authoritative air, saying, "Let me see your hands." I showed him as requested. "I knew it. How long since you rowed a boat?"

"About fifteen days." Except for the short trip across the cove, I had not rowed a boat since Newport.

The sergeant scowled, greasy sweat dripping down his forehead. "Your hands show calluses from using oars. I believe you are a whale boatman from the mainland. I heard you boast that you came to our village to find a place to plunder tonight. Isn't that right, men?" He grinned at the other soldiers. "You heard him, too."

I was shocked at the sergeant's false statements.

The officer looked at me with disgust glowing in his dark eyes. "We will hang you tomorrow."

CHAPTER 20
Fall 1781

The Tories wanted to hang me? Angered, I shouted my response to the sergeant. "There are laws, even among scoundrels. You need not threaten me with your gallows, for I do not fear it."

"We'll take him to the guardhouse and see how he looks on the gallows tomorrow." The sergeant rubbed his hands together and laughed as if he had told a joke. By this time, many of the villagers had come inside to witness my examination. Strangers struggled to get a look at me. One of the villagers, a genteel-looking young gentleman, asked the sergeant, "May I have the liberty of asking the boy some questions?" The man wore a fine velvet jacket and appeared to be wealthy.

"Yes, I will allow you to speak," said the sergeant. I saw that the soldiers respected this young man.

The gentleman asked me, "You said you sailed from Providence?"

"Yes sir." Perhaps this man could help free me from these mercenary monsters.

"With whom?"

"With Captain Christopher Whipple."

"What ship?"

"In a privateer brig of sixteen guns," I answered.

The gentleman asked more questions concerning my capture and escape, to which I gave true answers.

Turning to my examiners, the man said, "I have no doubt that this boy has told you the truth. I am acquainted with Providence and can tell he is not a stranger there. I suppose you will send him back to the prison ship. But if you allow him to go to my house, I promise he shall return in a short time. He must be cold and hungry after fasting forty-eight hours."

The sergeant grimaced but said, "Yes, Doctor, I'll oblige you. A sentinel will accompany the prisoner. But don't detain the boy long."

As the sun sank to the horizon, the doctor led me across the street to his house. "Wait in the doorway," he said to the sentinel. Inside the house, the gentleman told his servant to get me beef and potatoes. This was soon done, and I ate heartily. The doctor was absent for a short time. When he returned, he brought a quantity of warm clothing with him. "When you have done eating, put these on. Would you like some rum or wine?" I declined.

Once I put on the clothes, the doctor spoke to me in a low voice. "These blasted rascals will send you back to the prison ship, but that is the most they can do with you. I need not tell you to disregard their threats of hanging, for I see you are not afraid of them."

I nodded in agreement. The doctor scowled and turned red with anger. "These Tory mercenaries are stationed here to protect our property, yet they steal from us. Let me give you some advice. If you are returned to that prison ship, don't stay a day there. And if you should escape from Oyster Bay, continue down a country road six miles below the village."

By this time, the sentinel hollered for me to come out. The doctor answered, "In a few minutes." He continued in a low voice. "I suppose you must go. Do remember what I have advised." He gave me a silver dollar. I thanked him and placed the dollar in my shoe. He shook me by the hand and replied, "You are heartily welcome."

Thus, I left this patriotic and benevolent gentleman. His gift of kindness during turmoil calmed me.

The sentinel marched me down the street. Men and boys crowded around me and presented me with money. Some gave me a quarter of a dollar and others less. The guard hurried me along, displeased with this attention. I was touched by the generosity of these strangers, who most likely had little money.

As soon as we were out of sight of the crowd, a guard grabbed my money. I still kept the doctor's dollar in my shoe. The sergeant and three scoundrels joined us, marching me off triumphantly to the guardhouse about two miles distant. The destination was a long, low building with two square rooms and two outside doors. The first room we entered was filled with men similar to those who had been my guards. By the appearance of their eyes and the cards on the table, I assumed they were a drunken set of gamblers. I was a subject for these Loyalists to torment.

"What has he done?" asked one of the men.

The greasy-faced sergeant said, "He is a whaleboat boy from the mainland looking for victims to plunder. The lad says he has run away from a prison ship after being taken in a privateer, but I don't believe him. The doctor questioned the boy, saying the lad is truthful. But with all his learning, the doctor doesn't know everything."

A guard with rotten teeth spoke up. "We'll take care of him. This boy will grace our gallows tomorrow."

My rotten-toothed guard stabbed me with his bayonet to move me to the next room. He pointed to an old blanket on the floor in a corner. "Lie still on the floor." The guard gave me another vicious poke of his weapon. I felt sharp pains from his stabs and saw blood dripping from my wounds.

I lay down and thought about what to do next. Escape would be near impossible, so I tried to sleep.

Due to the thin wall between the rooms, I could hear the conversation in the guard room. One man said, "I bet a tankard of beer the prisoner gets away from the sentinel before morning, for he is a weasel-looking curse."

Another voice said, "Do you think Andrews would let him escape? I think he'd likely stab the lad to death first."

As I lay on the blanket, an army of fleas discovered me. The entire room was infested with them. The insects made their way through my clothes to my skin. It felt as if thousands of them, rank and file, were marching over my body. I rose halfway to kill the fleas. The guard ordered, "Lie still." He added profane language.

I said, "I'm only fighting the fleas. Don't murder me for that."

The guard jabbed me again with his bayonet. In pain, I watched fresh blood running from the wounds. Was there not an ounce of humanity in this man? "There is no honor in such cruelty to a prisoner. Have no fear, I won't try to escape."

"I'll show you the true meaning of cruelty if you stir again," was his reply. I was obliged to bear the attacks of the fleas without moving a limb.

After some time, my black-hearted guard was replaced by a pale sentinel who appeared to be more humane. I had a long conversation with him, as I could not sleep due to the stab wounds and the attack of the fleas. I complained about the other sentinel. Disgusted, the new guard said, "Some men are born brutes."

I fell to sleep at last, despite the fleas. On awakening in the dark, I was convinced I was back on board the *Jersey*. The wicked ship was grasping me by the throat, choking me. I was almost relieved to realize I was in a prison cell on Long Island.

After the appearance of daylight, I was sent to their colonel's quarters a mile away. A corporal and a file of men escorted me. Our course was over grass fields, which were laden with a heavy frost. Looking around me, I could still think of no plan.

When we arrived at the quarters, I was ushered into the presence of a colonel. He was a tall man of fine appearance. Near him sat a ship's captain, who was ready to sail for New York. When the colonel examined me, I repeated my entire story to the men. After my questioning ended, the colonel and the captain went into an adjoining room to take their breakfast. The men began a conversation, which I overheard.

The colonel said, "I think his story about leaving the prison ship is probable."

"Yes," the captain replied. "He tells everything right about the *Jersey*."

"You can take him back to New York and deliver him to the prison ship," responded the colonel.

"All right," agreed the captain. "We set sail after breakfast."

At this news, a chill traveled up and down my spine. I began to shiver, although it was not cold in the room. Was I going to be imprisoned again on board the *Jersey*? I felt deep within that I would not survive a second time aboard that ship. Up to this point, I had accomplished nothing in my life. I had never fired a gun or captured a ship as a Patriot. I had not avenged the death of my dear friend Josiah. My mother and family were hungry because I'd deserted them. Frozen like a block of ice, I could not move.

Before sitting down for his breakfast, the colonel came into my room and spoke to one of my guards. "Jones, take charge of this boy." The colonel ordered the rest of my escort back to the guardhouse. The colonel said to a servant, "Give this boy some breakfast." He turned to my guard. "Jones, keep a good eye on the prisoner. I give you permission to shoot him if he tries to escape."

After eating in haste, I seated myself before the fire. I took my shoes off to dry my feet, which were still wet from my walk through the frosty fields. With great effort, I endeavored to thaw my toes and my soul.

I was now guarded by a single sentinel, a tall mulatto. His musket was well-polished and, I presumed, ready to fire. My guard went to eat breakfast in the pantry, taking his musket with him. One of the servants, an attractive black woman, joined my guard in the small room. Giggles and laughter came from the pantry. Every few minutes, the guard poked his head through the door to look at me.

Even though I recognized the danger, I was determined to escape. It was possible the guard would shoot and kill me. But I was never going back to the *Jersey*. I would not die on that evil ship.

CHAPTER 21
Fall 1781

The guard poked his head out to check on me again. Immediately after he withdrew his head, I grabbed my shoes. This was my chance, perhaps my only chance. I crept through the kitchen into the next room. The outside door was unlocked, and I made my escape from the house. I ran through a patch of standing hemp near the yard, into an orchard, through a cornfield, and entered a wood. At every moment, I expected to hear a gunshot or a shout from the house, but only silence followed me.

As I stepped into the woods, there was a loud crack. A sharp pain in my back made me stumble and fall. I was captured, perhaps dying. No more gunshots came. I checked for blood but could find nothing more than a tear in my shirt. Thankfully, I wasn't shot. I looked back at the house and saw no one outside. My imagination had played tricks. Perhaps a sharp branch had cracked and struck me. I jumped to my feet and continued my dash for freedom.

Once I was well out of sight and surrounded by thick underbrush, I collapsed on the ground. I had run the whole distance without shoes. After removing burs from my stockings, I replaced my footwear. Shaking like a child, I thought about my escape. Thank goodness the guard had a woman friend and paid little attention to me.

After traveling a few hours more, I halted. Unless they used dogs, I was no longer afraid of a recapture. I proceeded east while keeping off the roads. Following the directions from the kind-hearted doctor, I traveled more than six miles. I dared not call on any house during the day, although I was quite hungry. That night I slept in a barn.

Early the next morning, I traveled until the growling of my stomach became unbearable. Looking for a place that seemed safe, I stopped at last. The door of a small house was open, and a strong, red-haired woman was sweeping the porch.

"Madam, may I get something to eat? Bread and milk would please me, as well as any food. I have money to pay for it." I still had the coin the doctor had given me.

"Yes, come in." As I was eating, the woman asked me, "How far are you traveling?"

The truth didn't serve me well, as I had learned from my previous experience. "To Sag Harbor on a visit to see my friends. After that, I travel on to New York City."

"I suppose you are not a rebel." The woman eyed me closely.

"Oh, no. I'm going back to fight against those scoundrels as soon as possible." Lying came easy to me.

"Do you think the rebels will hold out much longer?" Worry lines crossed her forehead.

"It seems to me they can't, for their cause is extremely poor. I hear they are almost subdued."

"Oh, yes. From the beginning, I thought the rebels would never last." The woman looked pleased with herself.

After I finished a dish of bread and milk, my hostess brought me more bread, but this time with butter. I partook of it freely. I imagine she gave me this dish in recognition of my supposed loyalty to the King. I offered to pay for my repast, but my hostess would not take a single copper from me.

"You are such a fine lad and devoted to King George." I feared she was going to pinch my cheeks in her pleasure.

I bid the woman good day and resumed my journey. I traveled from mid-morning until early afternoon. Much to my surprise, I encountered Captain Daniel Havens, John Sawyer's uncle, along the road. He was riding with several fine horses in the opposite direction. I remembered him well for hosting Sawyer, Rock, and myself in Sag Harbor.

"Captain Havens!" My heart filled with joy at seeing him.

"I am sorry, but you are—?" The man squinted at me for a better look.

"I came to your house with your nephew three years ago."

"Oh, yes. You were one of the three escapees. My lord, boy, what has happened to you? You look like the devil himself was after you."

I assume he spoke of my torn, ill-fitting clothes and the scratches and cuts on my face and arms. Briefly, I related my latest adventures, perils, and sufferings.

Captain Havens quieted a horse that was snorting and pawing the ground. "I'm going west, but you must stay at my home until my return in two days. I will procure a safe passage for you across Long Island Sound to Connecticut. Make yourself known to my family, who will provide well for you."

"Thank you, sir, for your kindness."

"To secure the safety of yourself and my family, stay inside the house. There are people in Sag Harbor you would not think to mistrust, but who would do us Patriots mischief." The captain shook his head and pursed his lips. "You cannot get to the town today. It is twenty miles to my house, and you will want something to eat."

"I had a hearty breakfast," I said.

"So much the better. You must travel seven miles and then stop. At that distance is a tavern kept by Mr. Snow. Tell the landlord I have sent you to his place to eat dinner. Here is a quarter of a dollar to pay for your meal."

"Thank you, but I have money."

"Take it and keep your coins. You may need the change before you get home." The man was firm in his response.

I took the money from the charitable captain and traveled until I reached the tavern of Mr. Snow. As I passed by the bar room, I saw two gentlemen whose appearance did not please me. Looking at their fine clothes, I judged them to be Tories. I stepped into the kitchen and asked the servants for the landlord. They directed me to the backyard.

In a low tone, I told the landlord that I was sent by Captain Havens.

"Fine, fine. Dinner will be ready in a few minutes." The jolly landlord gave me a ready smile.

"I have my suspicions about the two gentlemen in the bar room."

"Don't worry about those men. If any distrustful persons should visit, I will give you a wink to warn you. Let's go inside." As we walked by the bar room, the friendly landlord said to the two gentlemen, "Here is a boy who says he escaped from the old *Jersey*. He will eat dinner with you if that suits your pleasure."

I was shocked that the landlord was so open about my story. I half expected a Tory would grab me by the neck and shake me until my teeth clattered.

The two men must have been Patriots as they nodded heartily in response. One was an elderly gentleman and the other his son-in-law. By their speech, both were well-educated. "The older man pulled at his chin and said, "To think you survived the *Jersey*. You must tell us what happened." Food was set on the table. We ate our dinner, which was followed by an hour of drinking. During our time together, I related my adventures. While we drank wine, more company came into the bar room. A gentleman with a powdered wig entered, and my companions changed the subject. I looked to the landlord, who winked at me. I took the hint and left the room.

In a moment, the two gentlemen followed me outside. The older man gave me a crown. "We want to thank you for your service to our new country." The son-in-law nodded his agreement and gave me a dollar. When the landlord came to join us, I offered to pay for my dinner.

"No, not a copper." The landlord chuckled and waved his hand in dismissal. All three men wished me a safe journey home. After thanking them for their kindness, I followed the road on the island's north shore.

As dusk approached, I stopped at a farmhouse to inquire about the distance to Sag Harbor. An older woman opened the door. She had a full face with a noticeably large wart on her nose. As the lady seemed friendly, I asked, "Would it be possible for me to spend the night in your barn? Darkness is coming on."

"You may stay in the house unless you are a Tory." The

woman crossed her arms. "If you a such a black-hearted devil, then best be on your way before I shoot you."

"My father serves in the Continental army and supports the rebel cause." I decided against telling her all my adventures.

The woman gestured for me to follow her inside. "Then you are welcome to eat dinner with me. The men in my family are gone for a few days on patriotic duties. I am here with my servant."

I went inside the house and seated myself. The servant served me tea and an excellent meal of pork stew and apple fritter. After the meal, the mistress asked me, "Would you like a cup of hot rum?" When I shook my head, the woman downed first one mug of hot alcohol and then another. I tried to hide my surprise at seeing a lady drink so heartily.

"With your honest blue eyes, you seem like a young man I can trust. I'll tell you a secret." The woman gave me a sly wink. "You see, my husband is a smuggler. That's why he's away."

I'd heard stories of rebel smugglers sailing from Long Island. During the war, their numbers were increasing.

The woman hiccoughed loudly and continued. "The American merchants want the British gold, and the British desire the merchants' products. It works very well for all of us. And any extra money earned we pass on to Washington's army." Her eyes blinked and soon closed. The wart on her nose quivered as she began to snore.

It was time to rest. "Thank you for the delicious dinner. Good night."

The woman awoke with a start. "What? Oh, yes, of course. You deserve a comfortable bed." The servant conducted me to a room in the back.

After sunrise, I heard the woman and her servant moving about the house. She prepared a fine breakfast for me of hotcakes and bacon. As I was about to resume my travels, the woman tied up a handkerchief full of cakes and cheese. "You must carry this with you." I bid her goodbye and gave thanks for her generosity.

I sang a tune to myself as I continued my journey. Reflecting, I drew a contrast between my two hostesses of the last twenty-four hours. Although the women supported opposite causes, they had both shown me the most generous hospitality.

After four hours of walking, the houses and steeples of Sag Harbor appeared before me. Since my escape from the *Jersey,* I had traveled more than a hundred miles over six days. I felt like dancing a jig from joy but didn't want to attract attention. I was eager to leave Long Island and the British soldiers, Hessians, and Tory Loyalists who came jumping out at me from all sides.

Careful to avoid the notice of passersby, I walked through alleys until I reached the harbor. I hoped my friend William Waterman was also in Sag Harbor, ready to take a ship to Connecticut. Had Will also escaped from the *Jersey,* or had he met disaster along the way?

A small armed sloop was at the dock. An older man was smoking his pipe on deck. Perhaps he used his ship for smuggling, as this kind of vessel suited that activity. "Sir, may I ask you a question? Have you seen a young man seeking passage to Connecticut?" I described my friend Waterman to the master of the ship.

The seaman's voice was deep and hoarse, perhaps from

years of shouting orders at sea. "No, no one of that description has sailed with me."

"Thank you." I rubbed the back of my neck. I had hoped to find word of Will here in Sag Harbor.

On my way to the Havens' home, a young woman in a moss-green bonnet passed by me. I recognized her as John Sawyer's older sister. Rock, Sawyer, and I had stayed at her house as we escaped through Long Island. I addressed the lady by name.

Puzzled, the young woman asked, "Hello? And how am I acquainted with you?"

"Three years ago, your brother, my friend Rock, and I stayed with you."

Upon recognizing me, John's sister became tearful. "Come follow me," she said. We walked into an alley between some buildings, away from passersby.

"Let me explain my emotions." The young woman wiped her eyes with a lace handkerchief. "I fear I must tell you that my brother died a tragic death at sea three weeks ago."

CHAPTER 22
Fall 1781

I was overcome with sorrow at the news of my friend's death. John's sister told me the details, although she stopped from time to time to gather her composure. "Once he escaped from the *Maidstone*, my brother stayed on Long Island for two years. This past summer, he sailed in an American privateer from the port of New London. About three weeks ago, his privateer captured a ship. John was one of the crew navigating the prize to Connecticut. After the ship rounded Montauk Point, the captured crew of the prize mutinied and killed their captors." John's sister took a breath and pulled at one of her gloves. "My brother was aloft in the rigging when he was shot and killed. The recaptured ship sailed into New York City. We learned of my brother's fate from the newspapers."

I wiped tears from my eyes. "Your brother was a dear person to me. He was my companion under trials and perils. I found John to be intelligent and brave far beyond his years."

"Thank you for your sincere words," she said, her head bowed.

The war was taking away my dearest friends—first Josiah, now John Sawyer, and possibly William Waterman. Feeling useless, I stared at my hands. There was nothing I could do to help any of them.

After bidding farewell to John's sister, I found the house of Captain Havens and rang the bell. A woman answered.

"Hello, I'm Christopher Hawkins. Captain Havens told me to stop by your home. Three years ago, I was here in the company of John Sawyer and Rock."

"Yes, I remember you." The older woman stood in the doorway, not saying more.

"The captain mentioned that I might stay at this house."

The woman looked at the other ladies in the parlor, then opened the door for me to enter. I did not feel welcome. Perhaps these women were not comfortable due to the absence of Captain Havens. The only friendly one was the captain's niece, a slender young lady with dark hair.

"It's good to see you," said the niece. I'd met her three years ago at the Havens' home. Rock had drooled at her good looks.

Sarah offered me a seat in the parlor. "I remember you were friends with my cousin John."

I bowed my head. "His sister told me of the sad news. John's honesty was unsurpassed, and the generosity of his soul was unbounded. I extend my sympathy at the loss of such a fine man."

"Yes, we are all distraught with grief." The gray-haired woman shook her head and touched the lace at her throat. "And you? What brings you this time to Sag Harbor?"

I gave a shortened version of my adventures since leaving the *Jersey*. She gasped and held her hand to her mouth on more than one occasion.

Upon my conclusion, Sarah clasped her hands. "Amazing! You have shown yourself to be quite intelligent."

"Perhaps more lucky than clever." I had overestimated my abilities on more than one occasion. "It's now time I made my way home. I saw a sloop at the harbor. Do you know of it?"

Sarah smiled at me. "That ship will sail late tonight for Stonington in Connecticut. I will be a passenger on it. No doubt you can cross to the mainland in this ship with us."

"Thank you. I'll check with the sloop's master." Although Captain Havens requested I remain until his return, the women seemed uncomfortable with my visit. Besides, one day longer than necessary in occupied territory did not appeal to me.

I visited the sloop and told the gray-haired captain of my desire to cross the sound to Connecticut. He agreed to take me. "Son, come eat and drink this evening in my cabin."

As darkness fell, I boarded the sloop along with several other passengers. Captain Havens' niece Sarah was among them. The crew loaded numerous crates and barrels on board the vessel. The ship set sail an hour after sunset. All the crew and the mostly female passengers remained on deck. The faint moon hid behind clouds as we began our seven-hour journey to Connecticut.

I puzzled over the many females sailing on the sloop. There must be some reason for this. I approached Captain Havens' niece. "I'm amazed to see women on board a ship during wartime. I assume you are not visiting Connecticut merely for pleasure?"

Sarah shook her head. "No, hardly for pleasure. Not in the middle of a war."

"Excuse me if I overstep my bounds, but is this vessel used for smuggling?"

The young woman laughed, a light shining in her dark eyes. "Now, what would make you ask such an odd question?"

I looked around. "I noticed some of the women brought boxes with them, far more than would be needed for a trip across the sound. The hull is overloaded with cargo."

The woman tilted her chin in the air. "You are correct, we women are indeed smugglers."

Despite my suspicions, I was still surprised at her announcement. "I fear for the women engaged in this activity. What if you are captured or shot?"

Sarah stepped back and crossed her arms. "Do you think we seek pretty gold jewelry for our troubles? Women are not allowed to serve in the Continental army. This is our way of helping the troops."

I never guessed this charming and attractive young woman was a daring Patriot. "You are risking much by your actions."

"Any gold we receive goes to General Washington."

"And what goods do you have for exchange?"

"Food, clothing, medicine, and other such items. Come, let me introduce you to the others. None of us will be sleeping tonight." She grabbed my hand and led me across the deck. "Ladies, here is my friend Christopher. He recently escaped from the deadly prison ship *Jersey*."

In response, the women clucked and huddled about me. In answer to their questions, I told them of my escapades.

"Oh, how brave you are!" One of the young ladies patted my cheek. Another hugged me. My cheeks burned as I had never received so much attention from women.

That night I slept soundly in a berth but was awakened before dawn. I realized we had landed in a cove at the mouth of Mystic River. There were no buildings or other boats around the lonely dock. It seemed an ideal spot for smuggling.

On leaving the sloop, we followed a path through a brush wood to a house on top of the hill. The passengers had heavy luggage, but of what content, I knew not. When we arrived, the landlord of the house greeted us. The passengers spoke to their host warmly. He told me, "Get some sleep, lad, as there is still night left."

I didn't sleep right away as it was noisy for some time. I imagined the passengers were secretly stowing away the smuggled goods around the house.

When I awoke, no person was in sight. None of the sloop's crew or passengers remained. They must have already started the trip back to Sag Harbor. As I searched the house, I ran into the master. I asked him, "How much do I owe you for the stay?"

The master smiled. "It's all square. Sarah told me of your encounter with the *Jersey*, so I won't charge you a copper. Have breakfast before you start on your journey. Would you like some Pop Robin?"

"I know nothing of such a dish, but I'm willing to try." In a few minutes, a young girl set my breakfast before me. Pop Robin proved an excellent meal. On inquiry, I found it was cooked from milk and flour. The flour was thinly kneaded and then dropped into boiling milk with a large tablespoon.

Having taken my breakfast, I learned the distance to Providence was more than forty miles. I thanked my host and took leave. At last, I was in a territory controlled by American Patriots.

CHAPTER 23
Fall 1781

Rhode Island

I set my course toward Providence. During my long walk, I thought about my past and my future. I was lucky in my last escape, I knew. But what was next for me?

Twice I had gone to sea and twice captured. Did I still want to spend my life as a seaman? I had dreamed of being a sailor since I was a young boy. I loved the ocean air and the feeling of being adrift on the vast expanse of sea.

Yet I realized the limitations of that life.

As my mother had warned me, a sailor is at sea for months at a time. When I marry one day, will I want to be so far away from my wife and children?

I had little control over what occurred to me when I was at sea. The captain of my vessel was in charge of my fate. And if I served under a poor captain, such as on my first privateer, I was left powerless. Other elements sought control over me, such as storms and enemy ships. I wanted to be in charge of my destiny. Perhaps a life spent on land was not so bad after all. One day Rhode Island and the other states would be free of British rule, and I could have my own farm.

Although Patriot Fever had nearly caused my death, I still felt a burning desire to fight for America's independence.

Perhaps I would join my father in the Continental army. My battles at sea were over. It would take thirty armed men to force me on board another privateer.

I thought about my father, with his piercing eyes and often angry look. My added years of age gave me a better understanding of the man. He was stern but cared deeply for his family and his country. I feared, though, he would not forgive my youthful foolishness. I had fled from my responsibility to my apprenticeship and to my family. His disappointment in me might be too deeply rooted to fade with time.

During my travels home, a man overtook me on horseback. He offered me the use of his other horse. I accepted and rode for ten or twelve miles on a horse without a saddle. When we parted ways, my lower half ached from my ride. I continued walking at a slower pace.

As the sun sank behind a forest, I halted two miles from Providence. Seeing a man in the yard of a nearby house, I asked him, "Sir, may I take leave to sleep in your barn?"

"Yes, you may stay here," he responded. The older man had hair the color of snow.

To avoid questions, I told him how far I had traveled that day and how weary I was.

The man said, "If that be the case, you shall not sleep in the barn. You shall be as welcome as a lord, even if you have not a farthing in the world."

"I have money, which has been kindly given to me."

"Not to worry, I'm delighted to have you stay with me."

I soon learned that this benevolent, warm-hearted gentleman was named John Waterman. However, I discovered he was not related to Will Waterman. I told him I had recently sailed with Captain Christopher Whipple.

Shaking his head, the gentleman made a sympathetic sound. "If you sailed with Captain Whipple, I know your cruise was short."

"The last time I saw the captain was on the old *Jersey*. He gave me a message to relay to his mother."

"I can help you with that." Mr. Waterman leaned in and patted my shoulder. "My thanks to you, son, and to all our brave warriors. With your efforts, we will find independence."

"I agree." I rubbed my head. "But it's strange how the meaning of the word 'independence' has changed for me."

"And how is that?"

"When I was younger, independence meant complete freedom to do anything I wanted. I envisioned myself carefree with no responsibilities. But now—" I paused and searched for words, "independence will give me a chance to labor at my own choosing without interference by a tyrant. And I'll have the opportunity to enjoy my family and friends in peace."

Mr. Waterman smiled and nodded.

After a supper of cold meat and bread with blueberry jam, I told Mr. Waterman my experiences. When my eyes began to shut of their own accord, the gentleman said, "I know you are tired and wish rest." He showed me a bedroom, and I gratefully lay down to sleep.

After taking a good breakfast in the morning, Mr. Waterman accompanied me into the town of Providence. He led me to the residence of Mrs. Whipple, the mother of Captain Christopher Whipple. The woman's house was filled with fine maple furniture and portraits of her family, including a picture of the captain. I told Mrs. Whipple her son's message. With tears in her eyes, the fine lady confided she was grateful for my visit.

After leaving Mrs. Whipple, Mr. Waterman offered me money, which I graciously declined. I crossed the great bridge leading away from the city and turned left toward the north. Carriages and wagons squeaked past me.

"Christopher! You've returned from the sea." A boy I knew shouted at me. He was walking with two other young men I recognized.

"Yes, and I am alive to tell about it." The group of us continued our walk together as I told them of my escape from the *Jersey*.

A gentleman passing by on a horse overheard our conversation. The man was Olney Winsor, a merchant in Providence. "Excuse me, but you mentioned the name William Waterman," the gentleman said. "He is related to my wife. We've heard he was captured by the British."

I told him of Will's and my escape from the prison ship, but that I had not seen my friend since he jumped into the water of Wallabout Bay.

Mr. Winsor shook his head, and tears came to his eyes. "Poor Will. He has unquestionably drowned."

My heart felt heavy. I feared he was correct.

I traveled to Smithfield and to the house of Obadiah Olney, Esquire, whose service I had recently left. I found the farmer in his barn. The kind man accepted my apology for leaving abruptly and allowed me to reenter his service. Unbelievably, it was only three weeks since I last worked for him. Those days of my imprisonment on the *Jersey* and my escape were burned in my memory.

When I entered the Olney house, the women gathered around me like pecking hens. Mistress Olney patted my shoulder, quite pleased at my return.

Dorcas threw her arms around me but quickly backed away. "You were captured, and you could have died! And you never even said goodbye." There were tears in her eyes.

Her concern moved me. "I'm sorry. Do you feel I was lucky again?"

"More than luck, for you are quite brave, Christopher Hawkins." Her eyes spoke to me more clearly than her words.

Later I would calm her hurt feelings. I must admit I had missed Dorcas' ideas, laughter, and wayward curls.

Mr. Olney allowed me to visit my mother for the evening. At home, Ma threw her arms around me and did not let go. Although she was thin, I recognized her iron core. "Isaiah and Lydia, fetch the older ones to welcome their brother home."

My mother said to me, "We only heard a few days ago that you had been captured. Thank God you are home, and I don't need to fret about you anymore."

James and Silas begged to hear stories of my escape. I picked up a brother under each arm and twirled around. "Wait until after supper. I can only tell this tale once tonight."

An hour later, Stephen ran into our house and hugged me. I was surprised at the change in him since our last meeting two months ago. My little brother was strong from his farm work and nearly as tall as me. "You are safe," Stephen said, his face glowing with an inner sun.

My sister Mary entered next. Her eyes were puffy, and her hair lacked its usual shine. "I have been so worried about you.

Ever since I heard you were on the *Jersey,* I've had nightmares of that horrid prison ship eating you alive."

Ma gathered all her children around the table. She said, "Christopher's return deserves our thanks to God." We bowed our heads, and I felt a calm enter me as I thought of all my blessings.

After a month of peaceful labor at the Olney farm, I visited home at my father's request. In poor health, Father had returned home from the war to gather his strength. I hadn't spoken to him in five years. Even if he was still angry with me, the time was long overdue for me to ask his forgiveness.

I was dismayed at the changes in my father. The war had taken its toll, and he seemed far older than his years. My father was huddled in a chair by the fire, and I sat beside him.

"I hear you no longer are to be a tanner." Father shivered and wrapped himself tighter in his blanket.

I placed my hand on my father's knee. "The work was not for me. I prefer the life of a farmer."

"And to think you ran off to war when you were but twelve years of age." My father sighed, the sound echoing throughout his body.

"The desire to serve my country burned inside me. I learned about being a Patriot from someone near and dear to me." I nodded at him.

"I suppose I did often speak of my desire for independence." My father's stern look slowly changed to a smile. "How can I scold you for being of the same heart as myself?"

I smiled at him in return.

My father's hands fumbled for his pipe. "You've run away often in the past few years."

"I've had enough escapes for a lifetime. In the future, I intend to run toward something and not away from it."

I stood up and rubbed my father's musket hanging over the fireplace. He had used it to fight for liberty and our family. "Father, I'm sorry for the turmoil I've put you through. I did not mean to cause you pain."

"You speak of actions you did as a child. You are a man now. There is nothing to forgive."

When the little ones and my mother were in bed, Father told me of his harsh life as a soldier. "Colonel Angell is a great leader, but my journey has been a difficult one." His mug of warm cider wobbled in his hand. "And what are your thoughts of war now, son? Do you still believe it to be a child's game of seeking glory?"

"War is far uglier than I ever knew. My friends Josiah, John Sawyer, and Will Waterman have paid the highest price."

"And I, too, have seen many fine men fall." My father's eyes darkened to midnight blue as if enveloped by black memories. "But do you believe our battle to be worth the cost?"

"The losses are almost unbearable. But I'll never regret our stand against England. The dream of freedom is too precious."

"We will have an independent America one day." My father lifted his sagging shoulders.

His blanket slipped, and I replaced it on his thin frame. "Father, when you are well enough to return to the battlefield, I intend to join you under Colonel Angell."

"You've no more desire to sail the sea?"

"No." The highs and lows of my voyages flashed before me.

My bad luck at sea was overpowering. "I prefer to fight the British on land."

Father's trembling hand grasped my arm. "I would be honored to have you with me."

ONE FREEZING NIGHT IN FEBRUARY, I opened the door of the Olney home to check on the horses. With my face lowered against the chill wind, I blindly ran full force into a man standing at the doorway.

"Sorry. Did I hurt you?" I searched for the face beneath his winter scarves and hat.

The young man smiled, displaying a gap between his front teeth. "Believe me, Christopher, I've faced far worse foes."

"Am I seeing a ghost? Will Waterman, it's you!" I slapped my friend on the back so hard I nearly knocked him over. "I'm certain my employer will be pleased to have you as a guest. Do come in and have something to eat. I want to hear why you're still alive."

I introduced my friend to farmer Olney's family. "Here is William Waterman, my fellow escapee from the prison ship. He's returned from the dead." The Olney women, familiar with my stories, fussed over Will.

After we ate spice cake with cream, Will and I sat by the fire to share our stories.

"The last time we were together, I saw you drop into Wallabout Bay." I shook my head, still amazed to see my friend alive. "I was certain you had drowned."

"No, but I did lose my direction. I swam farther north along the coast than we had planned. The next day I was too exhausted to leave my hiding place in the woods. When I recovered, I searched for you on Long Island, but to no avail." Will rubbed the half-moon scar on his face. The crazy prisoner from the prison ship had left his mark.

"How was your journey home?" asked Will.

"I was recaptured by the British and almost returned to the *Jersey*." I laughed at Will's horrified expression.

All evening, we shared our tales of narrow escape.

One day, we will tell these stories of the American Revolution to our children and our grandchildren.

Juvenile Adventures of Christopher Hawkins Sen.

Christopher Hawkins' Memoir—the original manuscript found in the linen closet of Margaret Davis, mother of Peggy and Heywood (Woody) Davis.

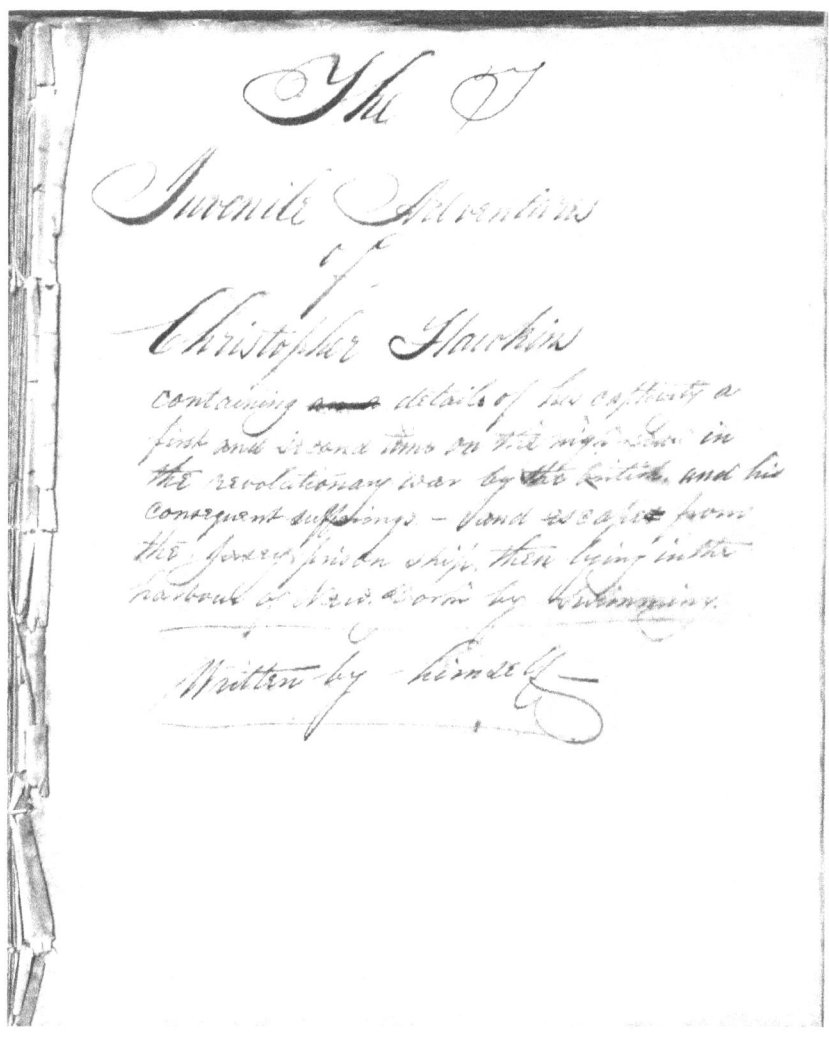

The Juvenile Adventures of Christopher Hawkins

Containing details of his captivity a first and second time on the high seas in the revolutionary war by the british and his consequent sufferings—and his escape from the Jersey prison ship then lying in the harbour of New York by swimming

Written by himself—

A Note from the Author

In 1965, my aunt Louise Davis was sorting through items belonging to my grandmother. In a linen closet, my aunt found a 70-page hand-written memoir by my great-great-great-great grandfather Christopher Hawkins. He wrote it in 1834 at the age of 70 and entitled his narrative *The Juvenile Adventures of Christopher Hawkins*. With more research, my aunt discovered that the manuscript was privately published by Charles Bushnell in 1864. The Davis family donated the original manuscript to the Museum of the American Revolution in Philadelphia in 2018. As a firsthand account of the Revolutionary War, Hawkins' memoir has been quoted and referenced in several nonfiction books on the war.

I am in possession of the family Bible that was owned by Christopher Hawkins, in which is written the names of his parents, siblings, wife, and children.

Through Bushnell's notes and historical records, I learned the story of Christopher during the years that followed his final escape. Christopher Hawkins enlisted in the Rhode Island line of the Continental army in Colonel Argell's regiment, the same regiment as his father's. Joining in March of 1782, he remained in the army for nine months. The peace treaty with Britain, signaling the end of the American Revolution, was signed in September of 1783.

Hawkins then worked at a shipyard and learned the trade of a carpenter. At twenty years of age in 1784, Christopher married Dorcas Whipple. In 1786, they moved to Herkimer County, in the state of New York. In 1791, Christopher Hawkins and his wife became the first permanent settlers of the town of Newport, New York. Christopher was chosen as the first Supervisor of Newport and held the office for 20 years. During the rest of his life, Hawkins labored as a farmer and carpenter. Christopher Hawkins was acknowledged by the community as an honorable man of good judgment. He was considered to be industrious, kind-hearted, charitable, patriotic, and to have a sharp sense of humor.

Christopher's brother Stephen moved to Newport and lived in a house near Christopher. On occasion, the two brothers constructed houses together. Christopher's parents and his younger brother Silas also moved to the area, where they stayed for the remainder of their lives. Christopher's sister Mary apparently never married and became a "tailoress" living in Providence.

Dorcas and Christopher Hawkins had a family of seven, with six daughters and one son. Dorcas died in Newport, New York, on January 17th, 1821. Christopher Hawkins died in Newport, New York, on February 25th, 1836, at the age of 72.

A few months before his death, Christopher Hawkins wrote a lengthy narrative of his adventures during the Revolutionary War. His son, Christopher Hawkins II, later gave the manuscript to Charles Bushnell, who published *The*

Adventures of Christopher Hawkins. In a preface to his memoir, Hawkins wrote:

> *My intention in publishing this narrative is confined to the attention of my children, grandchildren, and their descendants, with the hope that they will duly appreciate not only my own sufferings, but those of my contemporaries in the arduous struggle of my country for independence, in which success crowned the efforts of those who embarked in the American cause.*

Hawkins' original manuscript was written in the format of only one paragraph. I decided to write a novelization and adaptation of Christopher's story based on his memoir. I studied historical records, Robert P. Watson's book on the *Jersey* prison ship entitled *The Ghost Ship of Brooklyn*, and Charles Bushnell's notes from the publication of *The Adventures of Christopher Hawkins* for additional information.

One reason Christopher Hawkins' story is still known today is due to his description of and escape from the infamous prison ship *Jersey*. According to various accounts, up to 1000-1200 prisoners were kept on board the *Jersey* at a time. The number of soldiers who died during the Revolutionary War is estimated at 4000 to 6000, whereas the number of prisoners who died on the *Jersey* is estimated at 8000 or more men.

Some of the characters and scenes in my novel are purely from my imagination. I created the characters of Christopher's friend Josiah Greene, Captain Greene, and the laborers at the tanyard. However, Christopher's friends John Sawyer, Rock, and William Waterman were real people, as were the numerous persons Christopher encountered during his escapes. Dame Grant, who sold goods to the prison ship, was a real person. The officers and ships in my book were from Hawkins' memoir. As noted in the novel, Christopher describes in his memoir how he ran away from his tanyard apprenticeship, worked at the Olney farm, was captured three times by the British, and escaped each time. Hawkins wrote in great detail about his escapes, which I closely followed in my adaptation.

I am thankful to my ancestor Christopher Hawkins and to all the brave men and women who founded our nation.

Acknowledgments

My biggest thanks goes to my aunt Louise (Swigart) Davis for sharing her love of family history. She was the one who rescued the original manuscript of Christopher Hawkins' personal history, *The Juvenile Adventures of Christopher Hawkins,* from my grandmother's linen closet. She also brought Christopher's published version, *The Adventures of Christopher Hawkins,* to our family's attention. The Davis family donated the original Christopher Hawkins' memoir to the Museum of the American Revolution in Philadelphia in 2018.

I know the story of Christopher Hawkins will survive with the aid of my fellow descendants of Christopher Hawkins. These include my son, Ryan, and other Brownlee family members: my sister Anne Ovadia (daughter Sara), my brother John (daughters Julia and Peggy), my brother Brian (children Johnathan, Christopher, and Candice, and grandchildren Eleanor, Benjamin, Noëlle, and Milo), and my sister Karen. Our mother, Peggy (Davis) Brownlee, is the blood relative of Christopher Hawkins connected through her mother Margaret (Hodder) Davis, her grandmother Florence (Moon) Hodder, her great-grandmother Frances (Hawkins) Moon, her great-great-grandfather Christopher Hawkins II, and her 3rd great-grandfather Christopher Hawkins.

My Davis cousins will also carry on the legacy initiated by their mother, Louise Davis, and supported by their father and my uncle, Heywood H. (Woody) Davis. Woody is my mother's brother, and shares the Hawkins' bloodline. My Davis cousins include Tom Davis (sons Mitchell and Noah), Carol Krueger (children Claire and Davis), and Lynne Boyle (twin children Cecily and Brennan).

I will also acknowledge my other relatives who have descended from the Rhode Island Hawkins family. It would be wonderful to hear from you.

A big hug goes to my SCBWI writing group. Many thanks to Alyssa Cannon, Danielle Thomsen, Ruth Mitchell, Carol Cujec, Michelle Furtado, and Fran Shimp. They were a tremendous help and inspiration. We have so much fun together while we help perfect each other's projects of the heart.

I am delighted with Rebecca Barney for her lovely book cover and interior design, and with Staci Olsen's formatting of the book. I thank my friend Tricia Mendoza for her valued assistance in editing and my friend Bev Berwick for her kind feedback.

Here's a shout-out to the support given me from family—my son and daughter-in-law Ryan and Tati Becijos, my daughter and son-in-law Brandi (Becijos) and Rod Moore, and my grandsons Gavin, Haden, and Cian. Haden was the first young reader of my manuscript.

Finally, my love to my husband, Ron, who gave his artistic feedback and his constant support throughout the process.

You can contact me through my website (http://jeanne. becijos.com) and discover photos and articles related to *Christopher Hawkins and His Daring Escapes.*

About the Author

As a fan of family history, Jeanne Brownlee Becijos has enjoyed digging into the story of her ancestor Christopher Hawkins and traveling to New York, Long Island, Connecticut and Rhode Island to explore the roads Christopher traveled during his escapes. Jeanne has taught K-12 and college students and has written educational textbooks and award-winning plays. She lives in San Diego with her husband.

To learn more about Christopher Hawkins' journey, visit Jeanne's website http://jeanne.becijos.com

www.ingramcontent.com/pod-product-compliance
Lightning Source LLC
Chambersburg PA
CBHW060154130626
46556CB00006B/2635